Hearts of Gold Collection

The Becoming of Miss Blanche

GRACE HITCHCOCK

Published by Valmont House Publishers

Names: Hitchcock, Grace, author.

Title: The Becoming of Miss Blanche/ Grace Hitchcock

Other Titles: the becoming of miss blanche

Identifiers: Paperback 978-1-970675-03-0

Subjects: Christian Romantic fiction

All scripture quotations, unless otherwise noted, are taken from the King James Version of the Bible.

Cover design by Valmont House Publishers

Author is represented by The Steve Laube Agency

More From Grace Hitchcock:

Aprons and Veils Series:
The Finding of Miss Fairfield
The Pursuit of Miss Parish
The Enchanting of Miss Elliot
The Vanishing of Miss Victoria
The Courting of Miss Cady
The Making of Miss Matthews

Best Laid Plans Series:
To Catch a Coronet
To Kiss a Knight
To Win a Wager

American Royalty Series:
My Dear Miss Dupré
Her Darling Mr. Day
His Delightful Lady Delia

Heiresses of Adventure Series:
Miss Blaire in Blackwell's Island
Miss Wylde in the White City

Novellas:

Hearts of Gold, a Historical Romance Collection

"The Widow of St. Charles Avenue" in Second Chance Brides Collection

To my Dakota,
a true man with a heart
of gold

CHAPTER ONE

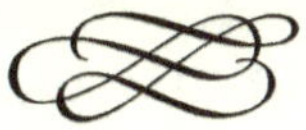

Las Vegas, New Mexico
July 1885

It was eerie strolling down the hall of the Montezuma Resort once more. Of course, it wasn't the exact same Harvey House. The last time Tacy Blanche had been inside, she had been running from the raging inferno that had taken the last of her family mementos . . . had consumed her earnings, leaving her practically as penniless as when she first began working at the Harvey restaurants nearly a decade ago—when she had changed her surname and abandoned her past. The freshly hewn wooden floors creaked underfoot as she followed the newly appointed housemother.

"And this will be your room, Tacy." Violet Trent paused by the last door in the hallway. "You will be sharing with me as you were one of the last waitresses to return to the Montezuma after the fire. I know it is a little unusual, given my new position, but the moment I received notice of your return, I had them move in a second bed for my dearest friend."

"Thank you, *Miss Trent*," Tacy smiled. It felt odd addressing her former second waitress as such, but with Violet Trent's promotion from Harvey Girl waitress to housemother over the working ladies, she had to do her best to remember to address Violet thus. She still dressed in her severe uniform, but no longer sported the large white bow in her auburn coiffure as the waitresses. Tacy shifted her small satchel on her hip. "When can I start? I'm rather anxious to slip into my uniform and get to work."

Violet's eyes widened in surprise. "Well,

I had thought you would like to get some rest after the train ride from Topeka."

"I slept on the train." *And if I don't work, I will remember how much the fire really took from me.* She set her bag on the bed and unpacked her toiletries. Her chocolate tresses would need to be tamed before work. Fred Harvey demanded nothing less than perfection from the waitresses of his fine dining establishments along the Atchison, Topeka, and Santa Fe railroad, and it wouldn't do to get off on the wrong foot her first day back. "I assure you, I'm completely able and more than willing."

"You never were one to remain idle for long. I have your new uniform hanging in the closet. We could use help placing the finishing touches in the dining room as we will have a new batch of guests arriving for the Independence Day celebrations tomorrow night, but, instead of having any arriving staff starting work right away, Mr. Harvey requested that the newcomers enjoy the resort for at least an afternoon. He wishes them to familiarize themselves with it for any inquisitive guests as they need to be able to offer an experienced recommendation to our guests."

"But I worked at the first Montezuma for nearly a year before it burned down. Surely, he wouldn't wish to waste wages on someone who has already been here." Tacy removed the modest, high-collared ebony uniform, fondly running a hand over the familiar gown. She had worked in it for so long, she felt out of place wearing any other gown, and if she did, it wasn't a bright color. She had long ago given up wearing such eye-catching ensembles.

Violet pulled back the curtains, flooding the small room with light and a spectacular view of the Gallinas Canyon and its mountains. "I thought to ask the same thing. While the activities since the original hotel burnt down are similar, you should study the grounds as the architect has changed the layout of the property. As you can see, even the location of the hotel has been moved so all can enjoy the rugged mountain view. Wear your uniform so no one asks questions if you wish to enjoy any of the entertainments."

"I'll change and be down at once." Tacy pulled the pins from her hair, setting her coiffure to rights.

"There is something we need to address before you go down—the head waitress position."

Violet's tone made Tacy's gut clench. She slowly turned. "Please tell me there isn't a problem, Violet—Miss Trent?"

"I know you were head waitress before our first Montezuma Hotel burned last January, but I'm loath to tell you that we were not able to offer you the position again, especially as you were unable to be here for the grand re-opening."

Tacy resisted the urge to flinch. She had worked very hard training new recruits in Topeka for the past eighteen months in order to move back into her position. The only reason why she was late was because she was recovering from a broken ankle that she had gotten from a clumsy Harvey Girl novice. "Who was awarded my spot?"

Violet gritted her teeth. "Felicity Chandler."

"Of course. Her father is good friends

with Fred Harvey," Tacy sighed, turning her back to Violet so her friend would not see her disappointment, and finished unpacking her few belongings. "I didn't stand a chance against her . . . even with a decade of work behind me."

Violet rested her hand on Tacy's shoulder. "I'm sorry. Truly, I fought it as hard as I could without being disrespectful, but our new resort manager, Mr. Rosehill, is eager to please Mr. Harvey, and he wouldn't challenge the idea for fear of—"

"I know you tried, Violet." Tacy pinched the bridge of her nose, and, as she did with any unpleasant memory, she shoved aside her anger for being passed over for Felicity and forced a smile. "It's fine. Really. I was late, and it would be unfair to remove the current head waitress."

"Felicity will need a second waitress, and I've named you for the position. Given your experience, I doubt the new manager will have a problem with that." Violet gave her a strained smile. "I must return to my duties. Do try to enjoy yourself, and I cannot wait to catch up over tea at the end of my shift."

"That would be delightful." Tacy dressed quickly before heading downstairs, pausing to peek at the massive dining room with its stained-glass streaming a kaleidoscope of color across the floors. Beneath the stained glass, the large windows overlooked the reservoir. Unable to resist her curiosity, Tacy crossed the large room to see what the view would be like. She had to admit, she liked this location much better than the first resort—especially with its proximity to the water. The property would soon be teeming with even more guests, taking in the curative hot springs and the delights of the resort during the holiday.

"You are back!" Ella Ashby cried from the doorway, arms full of ironed linens. "I thought we might have lost you to another more enticing Harvey House down the Santa Fe line!" She hastened across the dining room and tossed the linens on the empty table to embrace her former roommate.

"More enticing than the Harvey House with you? Never!" Tacy gestured to the sparkling dining room that was currently serving a late breakfast to one family in the far corner by the windows. "The architects outdid themselves."

"It's dazzling. With the layout, every guest has a beautiful view. Even our rooms have a view of the mountains, but I'm sure you already saw that." Ella grabbed a linen, spreading it on a table. "When I heard who the head girl was going to be, I feared we had lost you forever."

"In truth, I didn't know I wouldn't have the position until I arrived."

"Then you *are* leaving?" Ella's tone dropped.

"I've worked many houses down the line, but this one has a special place in my heart . . . despite the last day I was here." Tacy eyed the pile of linens, eager to make herself useful. First, she had to take in the resort. "What do you recommend I do to amuse myself today?"

"The mule ride up the mountain trail! They replaced the temperamental burros with mules. If you don't go now, you might not have a chance until your day off. Mr.

Tom Lane is still in charge of the trails and will be more than happy to take you."

JASPER CAFFERY GUIDED his horse up the steep mule trail beyond the Harvey House. He imagined that by tomorrow the trail would be packed with new guests seeking amusement. After using the trail for the past week, Jasper was comfortable to set out alone—even if the elderly guide hadn't been there to give him permission to do so. What was the point of traveling with his favorite mount if he couldn't take his mare out for rides, especially on a holiday he had never thought to take?

But his brother Camden insisted that a holiday would be good for Jasper after his latest, particularly trying, case that he had worked on behalf of the Pinkerton Agency for the famed Dupré-Dempsey sugar dynasty involving a wealthy escaped businessman turned criminal who had made threats against his rivals, the Dupré-Dempsey family.

So far, Jasper had failed in finding Wellington, making this only the second case he had been unable to solve in his career as a Pinkerton. Despite his unwillingness to take a holiday, the time alone really had been good for him, but if he didn't start working on a new case soon, he would have to find something else to distract him than the wildlife.

A mule shot down the trail, braying wildly and sending his mare skittering to the side. The mule was dangerously close to the edge. He darted past, eyes wide—an empty saddle on his back with the canteen on the horn slapping his side, encouraging the foolish animal to keep running.

He frowned. If there was a mule on the trail, so was Tom Lane, which meant a guest was potentially injured. He kicked his mount, minding the ledge. They charged around the corner, nearly colliding with a second mule. A flash of skirts was all he saw of the rider as the animal bucked her off. The woman cried out as she landed in a heap of black skirts, her brown hair tumbling from her little matching hat. He reined in his mount and leapt off, kneeling beside the petite woman as she groaned.

He drew his gaze over her, looking for an obvious injury before she lifted the black netting and revealed her face. His heart dropped to his stomach. "Eustacia? Eustacia Gibbs? Is that you?"

Her lashes fluttered upward. Her glassy green eyes slowly focused on him, her dark brows knitting in confusion. She pushed herself to sitting. "What did you call me?"

He grasped her hand, the touch sending a charge up his arm. It was her. No other had ever brought such a reaction. "Eustacia. Your name. How bad is your injury, Miss Gibbs?"

"Not bad enough for a strange man to keep holding onto me and calling me by a name I do not answer to." She jerked her hand from his hold.

She doesn't even recognize me. He ran his hand over the short beard he had grown in the past week. Was this why Camden suggested he vacation in Las Vegas? Had the man finally discovered where she had run away and sent him to soften the blow before Camden appeared? "Eustacia. It's me."

She scowled at him in return. "I do not know who you think I am, but my name isn't Eustacia Gibbs. It is Miss Blanche, and I need to fetch help for the trail guide."

"Mr. Lane is injured?"

At the name, her glare softened. She pointed up the trail, concern flashing over her features. "About two miles up the path. That's why I was in such a hurry. Mr. Lane was trying out a new mule that just arrived on the train. It got spooked and Mr. Lane fell and broke his leg."

Jasper rose and strode over to the ledge to catch the horse's reins before the mare's snacking drew her too far from them. "Allow me to escort you to the resort and fetch help. I cannot rightly leave you on a trail to tend to the man when you might encounter a black bear on the way down the mountain, Miss Gibbs."

"I said it twice and I won't say it a third time. I am not *she*."

She scrambled to her feet, whacking her skirts free from twigs, leaves and dust . . .

skirts that were just like the ones the Harvey Girls wore. She was a Harvey Girl? His heart pounded as pieces of her story came together. "I would never forget your fetching face, Eustacia."

She laughed without mirth. "Which means I have apparently forgotten yours. I don't have time for this. Mr. Lane needs our help." She fairly ran down the trail, black skirts fluttering behind her.

"Miss Gibbs! Take care." He swung up onto his mare and followed her. "Miss Gibbs!"

She whirled around. "My name is Miss Blanche, and since you made me say it again, I will recommend that you are removed from the property. Mr. Harvey protects his Harvey Girls and will not stand for any man being impertinent."

"You really don't remember me?" He certainly had not forgotten her . . . even her agitated tone still held the melodic cadence that had first caught his attention. He hated bringing up Camden's name for the first real conversation he had with her since that horrible day he had told her the truth about his brother. Maybe it would have been better for her not to remember him. "Perhaps it's the beard, but surely it is trimmed enough for you to recognize Camden's little brother."

At the sound of *his* name, she halted in her flight, her mien transforming to that of horror . . . then, resolution? "*Jasper Caffery*? What on earth are you doing in Las Vegas?"

He slid off his horse, patting the mare's mane. He was almost afraid to look directly at her, lest she run off again. "Until I saw you, I thought I was on a vacation from work."

She continued down the path. "Thought?"

"My brother suggested I take a holiday here, so I doubt all is as it seems."

He caught the tremor of her lips, but she focused on the trail before them. "No. When it comes to him, nothing is a coincidence. How did he find me?"

"I imagine he hired someone." *Someone like me, no doubt.*

"From what I remember, you were positioning to join the Pinkertons. Did you?"

She glared at him, accusations flashing across her features. She pressed her lips together and trudged through a patch of mud, not appearing to mind the filth that now clung to her skirts.

At least she remembers something about me. "Yes."

"Did you try to find me?"

"Since the moment you ran away, but you must know I would never betray you to Camden. After all, I was the one that saved you from a marriage with him."

She hiked her skirt up to step over a fallen log. "From what I know of Caffery men, you are not what you seem."

"That's not fair, and you know it."

"Whatever Camden thinks is going to happen, it never will." She shot back. "I will *never* see that man again. He ruined my life."

After you left, I felt the same. "I hope you do not feel the same about me. I-I much regret the way we parted, and I wish with all my heart I could have saved you pain."

Her pursed lips softened. "I know, Jasper. You were always a kind soul."

A kind soul? That showed some promise

over the disdain from moments before. The bottom of the trail was now in sight, sending his heart to slamming against his ribs. His request to see her again burned on his tongue, but he couldn't seem to release it. What was wrong with him? He was a man known to be without fear . . . until it came to Eustacia. He had too much to lose. "I-I am supposed to leave in a week, but would you allow me to see you—speak with you again?"

She sighed. "What about?"

"It's been a long time, Eustacia. I thought I might never see you again."

"Miss Tacy Blanche," she corrected, but with less conviction. "No one knows me by any other name besides the housemother."

"I know we must hurry to fetch help now, but please allow me the chance to speak with you once more?"

"I-I don't know, Jasper. I only just returned to the Montezuma. I can't take time off, or be seen with a man, no matter how innocent the intent."

He kept his gaze on her and his mouth shut. It had worked many times in the past.

Nervous people tended to want to end the awkward situation by whatever means . . . even if it meant promising something they didn't want.

"I'll think about it."

A boy in a Harvey House messenger's uniform raced up the trail atop a mule, the boy's legs flapping above the saddle that was far too large for him as he waved a paper in the air.

"This arrived for you, Mr. Caffery! It's from New York!"

Right on time, Camden. He thanked the boy and tucked the telegram into his pocket. "I need you to escort Miss Blanche down the trail and fetch help. Mr. Lane is alone on the trail and injured." He nodded to Eustacia, but she kept her gaze firmly fixed on the tower rooftop of the Montezuma. "I'll find you later, Miss Blanche?"

The boy laughed. "She's a Harvey Girl, sir! She'll be in the dining room any time you want to see her."

He chuckled. "Thank you, lad." He nodded to Eustacia and swung atop his mare, charging up the carved trail before glancing back to find Eustacia marching to the Montezuma as if she couldn't wait to get away from Jasper. His chest burned with the realization that he had found Eustacia Gibbs at last.

At a bellow from further up the trail, Jasper leaned forward in his saddle, searching for the man. "Hello? Mr. Lane!"

"Over here!" The man's shouting increased, the slurred choice words burning even Jasper's ears, but drawing him to where the older man sat sprawled over a dead bush, the dried twigs broken and scattered from his fall.

He dismounted and hurried to the man's side, fighting back a grimace at the unnatural angle of the man's leg. "Mr. Lane? Miss Blanche told me of your fall. Is there anything else injured besides your leg?"

"Isn't a broken leg enough? Blasted, cantankerous new mule must have sensed a predator when he bucked me out of the saddle." He huffed, shifting with a groan.

Jasper reached for him. The old man eyed him, but accepted his offer, settling onto the trail. Jasper withdrew his pocketknife and cut off the man's pant leg to access the wound. It hadn't broken through the skin. "Looks like you will be laid up for a while, Mr. Lane. Now, the question is, do you want me to set it, or wait for help?"

"I asked Miss Blanche to fetch help, and she won't let me down. Unless you are a doctor, leave it be, city fellow!" He gritted his teeth. "Already ruined my pants. I've had 'em for a decade! Saw me through many a trial, and here you go ripping them. Make yourself useful, and see if you can lift my spirits by telling me *real* help is coming up the trail."

Jasper peered over the side of the trail to where he could spot the roof of the Montezuma's tower, but the trees prohibited the details of the base of the trail. "I'm sure it won't be much longer."

The man released a string of complaints. "That's what my fiancée told me about marrying me, and what did Samantha do? Married a barber the next week, so forgive me if I don't believe you."

Seeing as the man would not allow him

to help, Jasper flipped open the telegram burning a hole in his pocket.

Jasper, by now you have discovered the real reason I suggested you holiday in New Mexico. When I located her at last, I knew you were the only one who could convince her to return to me. For better or worse, she always listened to you. If she doesn't, mention the diamond. Do this and all is forgiven. Camden.

"'Even Pinkertons need a vacation,' Camden said." Jasper scowled at his brother's words that saw him in Las Vegas for the grand re-opening of the Montezuma resort. "The lying skunk hasn't changed a bit."

He ignored the sting that, while he had failed in locating Eustacia, his brother had enough resources to find her. He crumpled the expensive telegram and shoved it into his pockets. He didn't have to follow Camden's orders. . . no matter that his influential reach extended to the Pinkertons. Jasper could quit the agency. He needed the money, and he loved the work—enough to move from the family's mansion on Madison Avenue to a small apartment away from his domineering older brother. This, though, was too much. The man had crossed a line—had tricked him into doing his bidding once more. Camden always wanted what he couldn't have. It didn't matter how many people he hurt in the process. He would get his way. He shoved on his hat.

"Do you see anyone yet?"

He peered again, hearing more than seeing a group make their way up the trail. "Should be soon."

"Soon? Thanks, Samantha." Mr. Lane shifted, gritting his teeth in pain.

"I could just leave you and seek out Miss Blanche's company. She was far more pleasant than you, and I'm guessing the mountain lions here are fairly friendly to you now that they know you?"

The man grunted, his face paling in his attempt to move.

Jasper laid a hand on his shoulder, halting him. "Can I help you?"

"Sorry, the pain is making me as cantankerous as the mule. If I'm honest, the worry is hurting more than the leg. I need this job, but now I got to find a replacement. But what kind of man would take on the mules knowing I'm coming back for the job as soon as my leg is healed?"

"I understand. I wish I could help you." Jasper scowled up at the majestic mountains. Even if he had been sent on holiday on false pretenses, the raw beauty of New Mexico was renewing after years working through family dinners and parties in New York City. So much for relaxation. Jasper already knew what his brother would do. With his refusal, a threat against Jasper's work would follow . . .

He knew his brother to be obsessed with the lovely woman. If Jasper did not comply, everything he had worked toward as a Pinkerton would vanish. Deciding to call Camden's threat seemed the best course of action. For now, he would allow Camden to best him if that meant he could stay near Tacy. If one thing was for certain, Jasper loved her today as much as he ever had, and he was not going to give up on her until she shoved him away. He rubbed his chin, his gaze resting on the taut face of the trail guide. "Perhaps I can be of service?"

"What's a city boy, like you, know about mules?"

He nodded to his mare. "I'm an accomplished horseman. What could be so different?"

The man snorted. "If you have to ask that, you don't know much about mules. Where is that doctor? This is a health resort, and I'm in poor health! You think he'd be faster."

Jasper shoved his hands into his pockets. "You wouldn't have to worry about your job being taken if you lent it to me for the summer. If you need a reference, you can ask Miss Blanche. We are old friends."

"You fancy our Miss Blanche, do you?" The old guide's face broke into an understanding grin. "That girl has her mind set on becoming a housemother one day. I am going to tell you what I tell every young buck who tries to go after her hand."

"What?"

"You've got a better chance striking gold in these hills than getting that Harvey Girl to marry you."

CHAPTER TWO

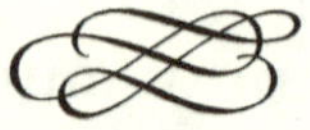

Tacy sank atop her bed with a groan, rubbing her throbbing ankle. She needed to be faster in her service, but her recent injury was holding her back. Her cheeks still burned over the fact that the other Harvey Girls noticed her flagging pace during the morning rush of the July holiday even though they had kindly helped her whenever they could. The day passed in a blur of greeting new guests, hundreds of cups of coffee poured, dishes served, taken, and so many armloads of linens changed that her back ached. She shuffled to the lace curtains, drinking in the mountains, and spied a little brown hare hopping into the shadows.

Throughout her day, she found herself looking about for Jasper, but as the hours passed, she began to wonder if he had gone on an excursion for the day. If so, she would most likely see him at tonight's dance before the midnight pyrotechnics show.

She didn't particularly wish to attend the dance tonight, but to refuse might appear surly—especially since the Harvey staff were already buzzing about the reason why her position had been given to Felicity, despite Miss Trent insisting it was only because of her late arrival due to a broken ankle. At least she would look put together even if she felt like elevating her feet on ice all night. She sank back atop the bed and returned to massaging her sore foot.

Violet closed the door, leaning against it with her eyes closed. "What a day." She shoved off the door, removing her hairpins, and noticed Tacy rubbing her ankle. "How is it?"

"I'll wrap it tonight for the dance. The

doctor said it would be sore for a spell, but I'll manage."

Violet shook out her auburn tresses as she opened the closet and lifted out both of their party dresses . . . well, Violet's was a party dress. Tacy's was her best and only one of two other gowns besides her uniform—a burgundy gown with ebony trim. The girls dressed quickly, giggling over truculent guests and their absurd requests as Violet arranged her hair.

Tacy finished the top button and frowned at her gown. She had loved it when she purchased it, but she couldn't help but think of her delicate robin's egg blue gown that had been destroyed in the fire. She had felt so elegant, and now . . . Now she couldn't afford such luxuries as seasonally bright gowns.

"I know just what we can add to bring a bit of color into your gown." Violet rummaged through the top drawer of her dresser, lifting out a shimmering blue ribbon. She moved behind Tacy and proceeded to pull out her hair pins. "A less severe hairstyle will transform your ensemble." She tucked half of Tacy's hair into a loose coiffure, woven into place with the blue ribbon, leaving the rest to fall in a waterfall of curls to her waist. "Much better."

"I'm not sure why you bother with such measures." Tacy murmured even as she admired Violet's handywork in their small oval mirror above the little vanity. "It's not as if I am attempting to catch a beau."

"There is nothing wrong with feeling pretty. Besides, it never hurts to look our best, even if it is just for ourselves." Violet winked.

Tacy dipped her head. She should have never confided in Violet of everything that happened on the trail yesterday, but Violet was the only person in her new life that knew about Tacy's past.

Music floated from the dining hall through the open window. Violet grasped her hand. "Come! We don't want to miss the festivities."

The women hurried down the stairs to the dining room that had been cleared for dancing and decorated with colorful, patriotic buntings, flowers, and streamers. The gaslights were turned all the way up, making the crystal glasses sparkle.

Tacy gasped, admiring how their efforts had transformed the area into a ballroom, guests already twirling in one another's arms as a string quartet filled the night air with a vivacity that touched all. "Surely the Montezuma can be seen for miles."

Violet nodded and pointed to the massive buffet table, laden with the chef's finest desserts. "I haven't eaten a thing all day just for this moment." She tugged Tacy along through the crowd toward the desserts.

Tacy laughed at Violet's aggressive weaving through the crowded room. The woman must have been starving. Tacy slammed into a solid chest. "I am so sorry, sir!" She looked up, the laughter bubbling in her chest fading at the sight of the broad-shouldered Jasper Caffery surrounded by a flock of ladies in their finest, brightest evening gowns.

"I'm not." His blue eyes sparked as he grinned, dimples appearing as he gently claimed her hand, and bowed over it. His dark brown locks were combed neatly into place, the scent of his pomade welcoming.

The nearest lady, a Miss Stanley, one of the more trying Montezuma guests, glared at her. "Well, I am. Mr. Caffery was about to ask me to dance."

His ears reddened, and he cleared his throat, clearly uncomfortable with the women clamoring for his attention. Tacy murmured an excuse and darted after Violet, her conscience stinging at once for not rescuing him as he was fairly pulled out onto the floor by Miss Stanley.

She and Violet snatched up a few confections, giggling as they snuck past the parlor and out onto the tower veranda. The breeze lifted her curls and cooled her cheeks. From her vantage point, she could easily view the wall of windows, spying Jasper whirling about the room with another lady.

"Are you going to rescue him?" Violet asked once her plate was half-eaten. She generously handed Tacy a spare orange macaron.

"Do I have to rescue him?" She bit into

the confection, closing her eyes at the burst of citrus flavor.

"You said he was once kind to you." She shook her head. "And it seems a right shame not to have his strong arms about you when he seems willing to dance with you."

"Violet!"

Violet laughed and gave her a little nudge. "It's only charitable to dance with him. Now, you go before I do."

She sighed and handed her empty plate to Violet and strode back to the dining room. The hullabaloo made her chest rattle, but she pressed through the crowd to where Jasper had returned from the dance floor only to be surrounded once more in a circle of ladies, all batting their lashes and fluttering their fans.

"Mr. Caffery, I believe you promised the rest of the dances to me tonight?"

The women seemed to draw closer about Jasper at her question, but he reached through the women to her. She grasped his hand, and he led her out onto the dancefloor. Their nearness to the orchestra gave her the excuse she needed to avoid conversation until the waltz swept them away in a circle to the other end of the makeshift ballroom.

"So, you remember me now?" He teased, but the light behind his eyes hinted at a hope that she indeed remembered their friendship of old—though short as it had been.

"Well, as you only just rescued me yesterday, it would be difficult to forget you. And about that rescue. What I meant to say yesterday was thank you for coming to Mr. Lane's aid. I'm afraid I've encountered far too many dishonorable cowboys in my time as a waitress. You are not one of them, and I apologize."

"Apology accepted." He whirled her about the dancefloor under the metal tendrils of the chandelier. "So, will you be recommending the mule trail to your guests?"

She chuckled. "Probably not. I prefer river canoeing to trail riding, for if I fall, it is much more forgiving, unless one is on the rapids."

"That's a right shame because I am

staying on as a trail guide until Mr. Lane recovers."

She stumbled over her hem. "W-what? How? I thought you were happy in your position as a Pinkerton."

He gritted his teeth, smiling as if for the benefit of others. "I didn't think I would be quite so unwelcome. But perhaps I overstepped. I've already spent the day as a guide, but if it is a problem for you, I can resign and return to New York. I'm sure I can convince the agency to take me on despite Camden's threats." He swallowed. "I don't wish to force my attentions on you."

With that offer alone, he reminded her of what he had always been—a kind friend. Her cheeks burned at her unkind prejudice. "Forgive me. I-I am extrapolating my hurt from Camden. You were never anything but sympathetic to me, especially since you were the only one to tell me the truth in the end . . . Forgive me?"

He wove around another couple and moved her toward the double-paned windows. "Consider it done."

"But whatever did you mean regarding

your position in New York? There was a threat?" Speaking *his* name was proving a difficult task.

He twisted his lips. "It matters not."

She followed his gaze to the bracketed ceiling and rested on the rather odd metal Art Nouveau chandeliers with their curling, vinelike fixtures and shades that resembled blossoms. "Seems like a threat that holds merit if you are staying here."

"Camden wished for me to bring you back to him. Even if I had to threaten you to do so—he mentioned something about the engagement ring you took with you, which would not hold up in court. I said no. He threatened my position, and I refused still."

She gasped. She shouldn't be surprised by Camden's aggressive play for her hand, but never had a man so quickly given up a life's dream for the sake of her own happiness. A happiness that had been built by her selling her tainted engagement ring . . . did Camden truly consider it not hers to sell? It had been a family heirloom. "Jasper . . . I don't know what to say."

"You don't have to say anything.

Camden was being unreasonable and does not think clearly when it comes to you." He shrugged. "I am hoping that by the end of summer, my position will be returned to me based on the reputation I have earned over the years. They need me more than I need the agency."

"But it was your dream."

His gaze rested on her. "Sometimes a man has two dreams, and one is far more important than the other."

She dipped her head, which was the wrong thing to do with all the people about them, but Jasper expertly guided her about the couples until the song ended. She moved to leave the dance floor, but his hand found her wrist, halting her.

"Will you come with me on an outing?"

"What?" She blinked.

"I know it's forward of me, considering how we only met a few times, but would you spend your day off with me?"

Her heart beat rapidly. *Should I trust him after my last experience with a Caffery?* She shivered, thinking about Camden's manipulating, narcissistic nature. But Jasper had given up so much to protect her, even without any promise from her. *Unless it is just a grand Caffery scheme for my hand. There is only one way to find out.* "Very well, but I can only promise this one conversation. After that, I think it might be best if we are to view each other as acquaintances. You have your work, and I have mine at the resort."

His smile illuminated his appearance, and Tacy had to keep herself from gaping at how a simple smile could transform even the most formidable of men into someone warm. She cleared her throat. "Now, if you'll excuse me, I need to check on Violet."

"But you will come back to protect me from the lady guests?"

She released a nervous laugh. "I'll think on it."

A PYROTECHNICAL DISPLAY sparkled overhead as Jasper disentangled himself from a conversation with a Miss Felicity on the tower veranda under the guise of fetching a cup of coffee. He couldn't keep himself from glancing about in search of the only Harvey Girl he was interested in pursuing. Eustacia had ignited a spark in him that was brighter than any of the fireworks blasting behind the Montezuma Resort that left the guests gasping in delight.

He felt a tap on his shoulder and braced himself with another conversation with a lady he had escorted on the trail. He turned to find Eustacia's friend. "Miss Trent? Isn't it?"

She bobbed a shallow curtsy. "Nice to meet you, sir. I believe you are searching for our Miss Blanche? She had to retire from a headache."

He frowned. "I hope it isn't too bad."

"I don't think so. It's been a long day, and I would kick off my shoes myself, but I must keep an eye on my girls." She cleared her throat. "And speaking of watching out for my girls, I must ask, what is your intention with Miss Blanche? With a tumultuous past, I must acknowledge any interaction as interest on your part."

His brows lifted, taken aback by her

question for a moment until he remembered that the Harvey Girls followed a strict code of conduct that left their reputation in the hands of the housemother. He touched her elbow and led her through to the parlor that held only two elderly couples seeking sanctuary from the blasts of the fireworks, judging by their scowls and the protests of every thunderous boom of gunpowder. "I assure you, I have only the purest of intentions."

She pressed her lips into a firm line. "I've heard another Caffery has said the very same thing."

"I am not my brother. I have loved her since the moment I met her and have not forgotten that love this past decade . . . even though I might have wished it away a time or two."

"Hearts have a long memory, Mr. Caffery. If you do wish to court her, it will take time for us to trust you."

"But you will approve my request to court her?"

"My approval will matter little if she will not have you. You must woo Tacy. I know her to be a woman with a heart of gold. She will recognize your heart soon enough if you stay the course. I will give you my permission to pursue her if she doesn't disagree. If I have even a hint of aggression on your part, I will have you fired so quickly it will make your head spin."

He grinned. "I would have it no other way."

CHAPTER THREE

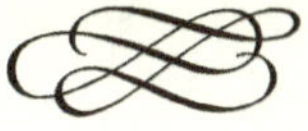

Tacy finished laying the fresh place settings over the crisp white linen when she caught sight of the table leg and swallowed back a groan from the thick green clumps adhering to the fine wood. She snatched her wet cloth, crouched low, and scrubbed where the little boy had run his snotty fingers along the leg. With it being a holiday week at the resort, Tacy had no problem finding second shifts in the dining room to fill her time and keep her mind busy. She had spent a decade trying to remove herself from the horrible memories of Camden Caffery, and with Jasper's staying on, it would be difficult to keep them buried.

She caught sight of a striking man in a well-tailored riding ensemble standing at the threshold of the dining room. It wasn't the first time a Caffery man stopped her heart. But she knew better now than to allow herself to trust too quickly. She scrubbed all the harder, keeping a wary eye on him.

The resort was already bursting with guests and all seats along the wall of windows basking in the beautiful morning light were taken. The only table vacant was by the door to the kitchen—her table. He adjusted his neckcloth and perused the tables, no doubt searching for an empty place. Even though he was an employee now and could eat for free . . . maybe he was willing to pay for the privilege of having a few moments to speak with her.

She stood so quickly, her elbow hit the table, jarring it, and setting the dishes to rattling. She clutched her elbow, tears stinging her eyes as she spun around so

Jasper Caffery would not see it was her as she gathered herself. *Thank God for these Harvey uniforms.* She had behaved abominably toward him last night, feigning the level of a headache when he had only been attempting to be friendly. It was only by her carefully honed skills of avoiding unwanted guests that she had kept from running into him all morning, or so she had thought.

The scraping of a chair on the hardwood announced that she had at last failed. She raced for the kitchen doors, the head waitress intercepting her.

"Miss Tacy. Where are you going?"

"Felicity, will you see to my tables for a moment? I—"

"First, you beg me for a second shift, and I generously give it to you, and now you want out of serving a table on the busiest week of the resort yet? No. See to your tables." She shoved her coffee pot into Tacy's hands, the heat of the silver pot hardly registering with the painful past roaring to life.

Beside her obvious flight, her dread was surely painted on her face as Jasper slowly rose, setting his napkin on the menu. She forced her lips into a smile and turned to him, and spying his cup kept upright in its saucer, she filled it with the coffee pot before recalling that given every table was taken and therefore, every Harvey Girl was busy overseeing their own tables, *she* would be the one making the cup code. Her cheeks heated at her unmitigated blunder. "Good morning, Mr. Caffery. What can I get for you? Hopefully, you wished for coffee?"

He returned to his seat. "I'll never say no to a cup, but I'm not entirely sure yet of my choice in fare, but how's your headache, Miss *Tacy*? Better, I hope?"

"I was able to tame it in time. Peppermint tea and lavender sachets did the trick." She nodded to the menu before him. "I'll give you a few minutes." She slapped her pencil down on her notepad and returned to the kitchen for a fresh pot, bracing herself for a conversation with him.

Felicity paused at the kitchen door with a stack of clean plates in her arms. "He's a handsome fellow, ain't he? Have you heard that Mr. Caffery is working as Mr. Lane's replacement? He's an improvement for sure."

Tacy moved around Felicity and refilled the pot at the urn. "Jasper? I hadn't really noticed."

Felicity rolled her eyes, holding the door with her back for Tacy to pass back into the dining room. "Not notice his broad shoulders, chiseled jaw, dazzling eyes, and full lips? I doubt it. I think we will see many of our lady guests sign up for the trail with him as a guide. There is already a surge of interest, judging from conversations I've overheard from the guests."

Tacy nodded and moved to return to her station, but Felicity touched her arm, eyes flickering with guilt.

"I'm sorry about earlier. I am under a lot of stress as head waitress, and honestly, I didn't expect it to be this hard."

Then maybe you shouldn't have taken my position out from under me. Tacy paused in her return, reaching deep inside for a generous reply in an attempt of peace . . . and perhaps in avoiding Jasper for a moment longer. "Think nothing of it. You spoke of Mr. Caffery's good looks. Are you interested in him?"

Felicity sighed, setting her plates equally apart on the nearest linen covered table. "It would be hard not to be interested in him, but a young banker from San Antonio is attempting to call on me. He knows that I don't want to leave my sister, so in order to marry me, he'll have to move." She shrugged. "I do not know where my heart is at the moment. And you? Do you have a suitor, or family nearby that saw you return to the Montezuma? I haven't noticed you with anyone before, so I am assuming you are from out of town like most of the other girls?"

"You assume correctly. I'm originally from New York City, but even if I could get back, there wouldn't be anyone there for me as my mother died a few years ago, and my parents' grocery store is no longer in the family."

"I'm so sorry. Was she taken by illness?"

"Yes." She had shoved aside the memories of her mother's illness brought on by the disgusting apartment they could hardly afford thanks to their sugar baron turned landlord, Mr. Wellington, signing them at a cheap rate and then slowly raising prices until they could scarcely afford food from their own store. And when they had tried to break contract to find another place to live, he threatened to sue them, and even if they did manage to escape him, he owned most of the apartment buildings in their area as result of his wild success in the sugar industry.

"And what about your father?"

"He's, um," she bit her lip, not wanting to confess how her father abandoned her after her mother's death, and in doing so, left many bills outstanding. The grocery store had been taken by Wellington's creditors, leaving her with no way to provide for herself. She had begged the creditors not to take away the last piece of her mother and allow her to run the store until the debts were paid, but they said Wellington wanted the cash now. She even went to Wellington's house, but, of course, she was never permitted to see the man. If she hadn't been given her first job as a maid by her pastor's wife, she would have starved . . . and she would have never met Camden and fallen in love. She shook her head. "He's away. I honestly don't think I'll ever see him again." She laughed to break the serious moment. "And speaking of never seeing someone again, I best get back to Jasper's table, lest he think I am avoiding him."

"I can take over your tables if you want to take your break now?" Felicity offered, reaching for the coffee pot.

She placed the pot into Felicity's hands. "Bless you." She raced out the door and for the grounds as if Camden Caffery were at her heels.

JASPER CHECKED the bridle of the final mule, his gaze flickering to the line of ladies dressed in their finest riding costumes lingering outside of the paddock, all twittering behind their colorful flapping fans that were making the mules' ears twitch.

Camden's threat came less than a few hours after Jasper sent his firm refusal this morning to convince Tacy to return. He shoved the threat into his back pocket. He need only wait until the day was over and Camden would see him fired from the Pinkerton Agency. His brother would be surprised to find that he was not as desperate for a position now that he had a job as trail guide with pay, room, and board. As of this morning, he was now bunking with Mr. Lane, which was sad as he wouldn't see Tacy in the dining room after today. Now that he would be eating with the staff, he would have to work harder to find out when she took her meals for a chance of a conversation and find her during his time off that would hopefully coincide with hers.

"Is the trail treacherous?" Miss Stanley approached in a crimson riding gown, her long train stirring up dust.

"Can be." From what Jasper had seen during his week of riding the trail as a guest, one needed to stay alert. "I've heard there are mountain lions and black bears, but they tend to keep away from the trail."

"But you'll protect us if they appear." She fluttered her lashes at him, eyeing his blue plaid shirt and biscuit colored riding pants that matched his vest.

"That's my job, and I happen to be an excellent shot." He rested his hand on the gun belt slung across his hips and put a pace between them. "My assistant will be bringing up the rear with a rifle."

She turned up her nose at the scrawny lad. "Seems the resort would provide a second man . . . instead of giving the position to a hobbledehoy."

"Markham may be scrappy, but he is better with a rifle than most men and knows these hills like the back of his hand."

"Markham! Help the ladies mount." Mr. Lane called to the assistant from his rocking chair on the front porch of the outbuilding that served as his home connected to the stables. "Caffery! Be sure to give my mule a carrot."

"Yes, sir!" Jasper tugged on the stiff Stetson. Lane had offered his own hat, saying it would give Jasper some much-needed credibility, but the stench of the old piece made his eyes water. He'd break in his new hat soon enough.

"Which mule is behind yours?" Miss Stanley ran her gloved finger over the top rail, feigning interest in the animals.

He nodded to a worn-looking white mount that no amount of brushing would make its coat shine. Miss Stanley expertly climbed the mounting block and perched atop the beast as one last guest joined them, a gentleman in a plaid riding suit with a stark black mustache that curled down at the ends and accentuated his sharp jawline.

Jasper frowned. He looked so familiar. He looked to his ledger for the name. "Mr. Morris Lessman?"

"That's me. I've been looking forward to viewing these mountains up close." The gentleman replied, his tone crisp and enunciated as if he were attempting to hide an accent.

Jasper tamped down his detective nature and checked off Morris Lessman as Markham directed the gentleman to the last free mule in the long line of women.

By the time all had mounted, Jasper was

already exhausted from the ladies' barrage of questions. Tom had told him nothing about answering leading questions. He nudged his horse and led the group up the trail that began as a gentle slope, but with every turn of the path, it was becoming apparent by the gasps of the ladies that his group was getting nervous with the height and lack of fencing.

"Mr. Caffery, is this quite safe?" Miss Stanley's voice wavered.

What had Mr. Lane said? "You are safer on the back of that mule than a baby in his mother's arms." It was a ridiculous claim given the state of Mr. Lane, but he had to follow the script. These ladies were expecting a western experience, not some tourist from New York City bumbling his way up a mountainside. With every cry of dismay, he called back Mr. Lane's favorite reassuring phrases until the women found for themselves that the mules were steady afoot, and they actually seemed to be enjoying the experience behind scented handkerchiefs. While the resort was in the finest of styles for even the most elite guest, there was no taming the wild beauty of New Mexico, nor the natural musk of the mules to an untrained nose.

He halted his mount at the first landing of the trail and dismounted. As each lady arrived, he checked in with them to ensure all were enjoying their time until at last the only gentleman in attendance halted his mule beside Miss Stanley. *Why does he look so familiar?*

The man shifted his gaze away as if surprised to see him as well. Did Mr. Lessman know him?

A cloud covered the sun and wind swept through the canyon, making the mules stir and the ladies murmur amongst themselves.

"No need to worry. The weather can be volatile, but it doesn't look like it will rain." He tried to assure them . . . but being rather new to the terrain himself, he was only following the script Mr. Lane had given him. What did he know about reading the weather? "Shall we continue our journey up the mountain?"

"Of course, Mr. Caffery," answered Miss Stanley, batting her lashes to him. She turned her mule to regain the position directly behind his horse.

They continued up the path when the heavens opened and drenched them. The ladies cried out and all admiration for their so-called rugged guide fled.

CHAPTER FOUR

After two days of rain, the sun finally banished the gray clouds, which greatly improved Tacy's mood as she could spend her day off walking the gardens or read out of doors in peace instead of being cooped up in the upstairs Harvey Girl parlor where she could barely get through a sentence without a girl squealing about something and interrupting her concentration.

Selecting a beautifully bound emerald book with gold lettering from the Montezuma's library, Tacy slipped outside to her old favorite reading spot that had been spared the renovations of the new Harvey resort. Tacy carefully gripped the book in her teeth and climbed up the giant live oak, the familiar scrape of the rough bark against her skin welcoming her home. Nestling atop a massive dipping branch with her back against the trunk, she lost herself in the book of poems, sighing with delight as a bird sang in the branches of her tree, lulling her to close her eyes for only a moment.

She gradually became aware of the trunk of the tree sliding away as she plummeted. She gasped, bracing herself for the ground. One arm encircled her waist and the other swept under her legs. She slammed against a muscular chest, knocking them both into the tall grass. The man released a grunt as she landed atop him.

She pressed her hands to his chest, lifting her head, gasping at the nearness of his lips to hers. "Jasper?"

"You okay?" He squeezed out.

She nodded, brushing back a lock of his dark hair, looking for an injury. "Are you hurt?"

He coughed, a half-smile playing at his lips. "Maybe if you got off me, I could tell."

Her cheeks at once burst into flames as she scrambled off him, mortified that she had not done so the very instant she landed.

He slowly sat up, gingerly testing his limbs. "No harm done. I didn't know you enjoyed tree climbing."

"Tree *reading* actually. It's an art which should not be conducted while lethargic. What brings you out this way? Is my reading spot not quite so secret?"

"Well, I *am* a Pinkerton." He winked as he rose, holding out his hand to her. "Actually, I spoke with Miss Trent, and she said that you have the rest of the day off. And seeing as the ground is far too muddy for a trail ride, I made the decision to close the trail until tomorrow."

She snatched up her book, turning it over, and sighed in relief that none of the pages had been bent. She dusted off the cover, staring up at him. "So, what are you going to do on your day off?"

"You mentioned that you enjoyed the

river, and I had thought that you might want to attempt canoeing with me. Then the rain started. Perhaps I could take you hiking instead." He lifted the two long walking sticks that he must've dropped in his attempt to catch her. "I checked one of the paths and found it to be surprisingly well intact after the rainfall."

Hiking? The man truly did not know her. Riding, yes, walking, yes, but an incline that left one panting for breath from a pinching corset while evading sharp rocks. . . nothing could make that enjoyable. *But, if Jasper makes even hiking enjoyable, it might be a sign that allowing him to pursue me is the right path.* "When?"

"How's now?" He nodded to her shoes. "Are those serviceable enough?"

"They are my most sensible." She rose and arched her back. Her simple bustle was not ideal for the trail, but at least her skirts had a sensible hem, lacking the long train most women sported. After the fire, she had determined that her dresses had to last and would be made over as the fashion changed, which did not allow for flowing trains. "And as for my gown, I don't have anything else to wear besides the gown you saw me in for the holiday."

At that confession, his brows rose for only a moment before he erased his surprise. He handed her the stick that reached her shoulders. "Shall we?"

"Why not?" Hopefully, she would not live to regret breaking her one Western rule —no avoidable hiking. What could go wrong?

HER BREATHS WERE SOUNDING MORE labored, but she did not utter a complaint. She was unchanged in that manner. He paused where the path consisted of jagged rocks piercing through the dirt, which could lead to a nasty fall. He extended his hand to her. "We are almost to the summit."

She glanced up, huffing, cheeks red from the exertion, and her brown locks pasted to the side of her face from the perspiration gathered there. She was still the loveliest woman he had ever beheld. She eyed his hand and tentatively placed her hand in his, releasing him the moment she had crossed over the stones.

"Shall we pause a moment, Miss Blanche?" The name still felt foreign on his tongue as he had only thought of her as Eustacia Gibbs for the past decade.

"Oh, thank the good Lord." She sank beneath a scraggly cedar tree, reaching for her canteen strap and gulping the water he had brought for her.

He ran his hand over his mouth to hide his laughter. The hike hardly had an incline, and here she was panting like she had scaled a mountain. He waited, sipping from his own canteen as the high-pitched call of downy woodpeckers filled the air. A raccoon chittered nearby.

Eustacia held a finger to her lips and pointed. He followed her finger to where he spied the raccoon's beady eyes watching them in anticipation of an easy morsel. Jasper reached into his pocket and withdrew a pastry bag with the scone he had brought for a treat.

"I wouldn't feed him if I were you." Eustacia warned softly.

"I caught you from falling out of a tree. I think I can protect you from one raccoon." He chuckled and tossed a crumb toward the animal, encouraging him to come closer. He had seen a raccoon only a handful of times, and this close encounter was made all the more special by sharing it with Eustacia who eyed him with a side smirk as the animal snatched it up with a victorious purr, gobbling it in one bite.

Jasper tore off another piece and tossed it to him. "So, it seems hiking is not your first choice of a pastime. Tell me, what do you like to do for enjoyment?"

She wrinkled her nose and stared up at him, blinking in the sunlight. "Well, usually I am too tired to be doing much of anything, but I love taking ambles out to somewhere I can't hear any other person, and I can be alone with a good book to keep me company."

"Ah yes, tree reading, a novel pastime. What kind of books?"

She tilted her head. "Why?"

He crossed his arms with a smile playing on his lips. "I've waited a long time for the privilege of a conversation with you."

"It's that Pinkerton side of you that won't just let matters lie." She clicked her tongue with a teasing smile. "Why do you care?"

"Because I like you, Miss Blanche."

She picked up a twig and broke it into small pieces. "*Jane Eyre* is a favorite."

He nodded. "Mmm, yes—a great piece of literature."

"You've read it?" Her brows rose.

"Well, I'm not much of a reader, but if I were, I'm certain I'd be quite well read, and *Jane Eyre* would be one of the first of many books that I would devour."

She laughed, the beautiful sound filling the air, and he determined to make her laugh more. "Well, what do *you* do for enjoyment, Jasper?"

"As a Pinkerton, my job is what I used to love. I lived and breathed being a

Pinkerton." He shook his head. "Regardless, I'm growing weary of being put in situations that I have little ability to change, and my calluses that I've had to keep for so long have been worn down to the bone, and the tough choices are beginning to take too great a toll—along with choices that have been forced upon me. It takes a lot out of you, and it keeps me from having the one thing I've been missing."

"Which is?" She pointed to a second raccoon approaching the first.

"A family."

"Surely the Pinkerton Agency isn't requiring you to leave behind a chance of a family?"

"Not really." He tossed a few pieces before the animals, laughing as they pounced. It was too early to tell her that he had fallen in love with her the moment he met her . . . that when he had told her of his brother's secret, it hadn't been with the purest of intentions—he had wanted her to leave Camden. He had never thought that she would run so far, nor forget him in the process. He supposed he deserved it. "So, tell me a little more about your family."

She frowned.

"We were friends once."

"Briefly."

"Briefly enough that I wished to know everything about you."

She swiveled toward him. "Why on earth?"

"Because, Miss *Blanche,* you fascinate me."

She pressed her lips together, studying him as if to determine his intentions with the question. "My mother died from tuberculosis that she contracted from our apartment in New York."

"I was sorry to discover that in my search for you. You said your father was away. Where is he now?"

"It's complicated and would take a long time to explain."

"I know what you mean. I have a rather complicated family story as well."

"I would be inclined to agree with that." She crossed her arms.

That would not do. "Shall we keep going? I want to reach the summit before too long so we can return by dinner."

She swallowed, green eyes wide. "I hope you brought more food."

"I have a sandwich for us to split in the other pocket."

"Good, because we are surrounded." She lifted a finger, pointing out five massive raccoons surrounding them, all baring their teeth and raising their surprisingly menacing little hands. "And they look hungry."

"I thought raccoons were supposed to be cuddly." Jasper slowly rose with Eustacia's hand gripped in his. "These fellows are twice the size of our first friend!" He kicked at one getting too close, and it hissed.

She jerked Jasper back. "Don't do that! They could have rabies. And besides, they just want the food you promised them."

He gritted his teeth and slowly reached inside his pocket, lifting out the beautiful sandwich wrapped in wax paper. The animals leapt for them. Eustacia screamed as Jasper lost all thought but to run with her. He grasped her hand, and they bolted, the raccoons following too closely behind for comfort.

"Drop the sandwich! Drop it!" Eustacia squealed as one nipped at her ankles.

Jasper turned, still running backwards, and launched the sandwich as far from them as he could manage, a piece of ham flying out, interesting the nearest ones enough to halt their attack as he and Eustacia ran for the hills.

CHAPTER FIVE

"Who knew raccoons were so aggressive?"

"They're not usually, unless . . ." She crossed her arms, giving him a knowing glance, "the *tourists* have been feeding them, and when you did not provide them all fare, they grew angry."

At the distant chattering, Jasper started, sending her into peals of laughter.

"Rabies is not a laughing matter. I'm pretty sure one was foaming at the mouth!"

"He had a Harvey House pastry on the line—I'd be foaming at the mouth over those too."

Tacy balanced on the small boulder in

the creek, attempting to reach the other side. Being with Jasper was confusing. He looked like Camden, moved like him—but that is where the similarities ended. This man was interested in her day. He was genuinely caring. Camden had hated that she was from a poor family, that her mother died from a disease brought on by their moldy apartment, that her father left her . . . so much so that Camden had attempted to keep their impending marriage a secret and even refrained from asking much about her past after the first few unfavorable answers.

Her foot slipped on a rock, and she cried out as she fell toward the creek. Jasper's hand at once grasped her elbow, pulling her up against him, steadying her.

"Are you all right?" He whispered into her hair.

She pushed herself out of his arms, not minding that her foot sank into the water as she did so. She could not afford to be caught in his arms after all the work she did to repair her reputation. "Didn't hurt a bit."

His dark gaze met hers. "That's not why I was asking." He halted. "I had hoped the awkwardness would pass, but unless we air out the past, there will always be Camden between us."

"Us?" She snorted. "There is no us, Jasper."

He grasped her hand, gently halting her flight. "But I'd like there to be."

She crossed her arms.

"You've known of my feelings since the day we met. Why else would I still be here when I should be back in New York fighting for my position, but to stay by your side?"

"Why, the wonderful amenities the Montezuma has to offer, of course, like delightful pastries and sandwiches." She laughed, attempting to break the seriousness clouding the air.

"Eustacia. Please."

She shouldn't look into his eyes, but she could not help it. The moment he held her gaze, she felt her defenses threatened and her soul comforted all at once. "What your brother did was unthinkable . . . and I never had a moment to tell you how I felt in your helping me. I never thanked you."

"I am not looking for your thanks. It was

the right thing to do, and I would have done it for anyone."

"Well, it meant the world to me." She planted her hands on her hips and studied the horizon. "Are we almost to the summit?"

"Yes, but—"

She didn't wait for the rest of his answer and marched up the path, panting as they reached the end of the trail. It was breathtaking. They stood looking out until a cloud covered the sun. Droplets fell.

"Again?" Jasper gritted his teeth. "I'm sorry, Eustacia."

"Why? Did you call the rain clouds?"

"Maybe. Every time I'm on this mountain, it seems I do. But I should have been paying better attention. We better head back. I never can tell how hard it's going to pour."

The rain made the journey down slick, and she felt her feet slide out from under her, despite her walking stick.

"Eustacia!" Jasper dove toward her, his hand grasping her head before it struck a stone. "Are you hurt?"

She shook her head, dazed more by his

touch than her fall. "Just embarrassed. I've never been so clumsy in my life. Tumbling not once, or twice, but three times." She scrambled to her feet, crying out in pain.

"What is it?"

"My ankle. I think I twisted it." She rubbed it, praying it was not worse than a twist . . . she couldn't afford for her ankle to relapse.

He looked to her and to her skirts. "May I?"

She snorted, shifting away from him. "Are you a doctor now?"

"Do you realize that you are the second person to ask me that since my arrival?" He chuckled. "I was trained in the most basic of doctoring should I, or one of my agents, become injured on the job."

She nodded, and he lifted her hem to the top of her boot and gently slid it off as Tacy swallowed a cry. The rain began in earnest, soaking them both as Jasper replaced her shoe.

"Not broken, but I don't think you should be walking on it."

She shrugged, laughing. "I'm afraid I do not have that luxury on a hike."

"As the trail guide, it is my duty to see you safely back to the resort. We best be hurrying down, and a hurt ankle does not allow that and might actually hurt you further." He swept her into his arms. "The only sensible option is to carry you."

"Jasper!" She threw her hands about his neck instinctively, and once they were there, she realized she could not remove them without causing him greater discomfort in holding her. She simply had to endure the proximity.

They rounded the path, and she drew in a sharp breath at the sight of the gang of raccoons huddled under a cedar, teeth bared.

"Uh oh . . . I think I may have been right about the rabies," Tacy whispered. "These animals aren't acting right."

HE WALKED BACKWARDS, facing the animals—waiting for them to pounce. The moment they were out of sight of the beasts, he sprinted down the mountain as the rainfall abated. At last, he paused, gasping for breath. Eustacia was light, but running downhill with her was taxing. He set her down and rested his hands on his knees, breathing deeply.

She rubbed her ankle. "I can't believe you ran with me."

"*And* protected you from feral raccoons." He gasped for breath. "Don't forget that gallant part in your regaling tales of my heroism. I think that earns me one question."

She giggled. "I suppose it is only fair when you put it that way."

"Why did you run without saying goodbye?"

"It wasn't because I didn't want to. I was afraid of what Camden might do if he had any information on me." She shook her head. "You know how obsessive he is, especially when he doesn't get his way. I thought he loved me until you came along and exposed his love for what it really was."

Jasper kicked at a fallen branch. "Do you resent my telling you the truth?"

"Resent?" She laughed. "You saved my life, Jasper Caffery."

A shot rang out. Jasper pulled her down to the ground and instinctively reached for his pistol before remembering they were in the wild, and hunters no doubt roamed the area. "Stay your fire!"

A man appeared at the edge of the trail in a ridiculous emerald and gold hiking suit with a rifle at the ready. "My apologies! I wandered away from the trail in hopes of a bit of hunting."

It was the fellow from the mule ride, Mr. Lessman. "If it is hunting you wish for, speak with the game warden," Jasper scolded.

"Are you folks unharmed?" He nodded to Eustacia. "I hope my shot did not startle you into an injury?"

"The lady twisted her ankle on our hike, but otherwise, we are unharmed."

"I say! What bad luck." Mr. Lessman strode to their side. "I shall join you in returning to the Montezuma. It will be a relief to get out of these wet clothes."

Jasper rose, holding his arms out to Eustacia. With a half-smile, she lifted her arms to him. Hiking down with her cradled in his arms would have been a dream, if not for the gentleman who prattled on and on. At Jasper's grunt of annoyance, the fellow eyed Miss Blanche.

"Shall I carry her for a spell? I dare say she is light enough for me."

Her arms tightened around his neck, sending a surge of protectiveness through his heart. "No, thank you. We are quite near the base of the trail."

At the bottom of the mountain, Mr. Lessman grasped Eustacia's hand. "It was a pleasure getting to know you, Miss Tacy. Take care of that ankle." He tipped his hat and trotted away with more energy than Jasper would suppose of a man of his years.

Jasper set her down on the bench the trail guides had set up for returning hikers.

"Did you enjoy the trail, besides getting hurt?"

Her lips quirked. "I've never particularly liked hiking, but you almost made it enjoyable."

"Almost?" He laughed. "Such glowing praise might stop a man's heart."

"I'm afraid nothing can make hiking fun, but I'm sad to return to work, and I'm never sad about that."

"Now, *that* is praise. What about a picnic on your next free day?" He braced himself. She could say no. She could walk away right now and never look back—what with Camden knowing her location, he wouldn't blame her. *He hasn't shown up yet . . .*

"Very well." She scooted off the bench and tested her ankle, her brows raising. "It's not nearly as bad now."

"Thank goodness, but if you feel any pain, I could carry you into the resort."

"I can't afford any more time off, and if they see me in your arms, I better have a good excuse." She laughed. "The Harvey House code of conduct would only allow you to carry me if my ankle was truly hurt. However, I will accept the support of your arm."

"Despite my wishing to keep you in my arms, I am grateful it was only a twist," Jasper said as they approached the steps of the Montezuma. "I really enjoyed spending the day with you. I was hoping you would allow me to call on you?"

"I've already said yes to a picnic." She smiled up at him.

"Yes, but I want this picnic to be more than just a meal shared by friends."

She picked dirt off her sleeve, worrying her bottom lip. He rested his hand atop hers, stilling her busy work and lifted her chin to meet his gaze, praying she would trust him with her heart.

"You'd have to ask Miss Trent, but if she says yes, I would not be opposed."

His heart soared. "Eustacia, I—"

"How are you enjoying your new position, brother?"

CHAPTER SIX

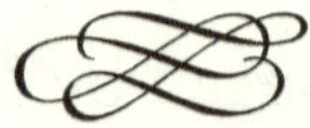

She whirled around, her hands flitting to her mouth. The years of fear of being discovered and dragged back into a painful past flooded her being. This was no nightmare. "C-Camden?"

"So, this is why you said no, Jasper . . . even at the cost of your precious position. I always knew you wanted my fiancée for yourself." Camden strode down the steps of the resort.

She glanced about, sighing in relief that the porch was vacant. It must be the main lunch hour, which meant there was a wall of windows above them that could witness their interaction. If only she were still on the isolated path, she could have this conversation away from any prying eyes in the dining room. She kept her face blank.

"I'd do it again if it meant protecting her from you." Jasper's fists clenched as he closed the distance between himself and Tacy.

"I meant her no harm . . . I never did." Camden's gaze flitting over Tacy. "I do not know how it is possible that you have become an even lovelier woman since we parted—a parting that has grieved me for a decade." He reached for her hand.

For some reason, she allowed him to take it—to draw her away from Jasper. His touch no longer inspired the fire to spark up her arm as it once had and never the way Jasper's touch sent her heart to skipping. "What are you doing here, Camden?"

"What I never stopped doing—chasing you." He shook his head. "You left that day in such a hurry, you never gave me a chance to explain."

"What are you hoping to achieve by being here? What was there to explain?" She tugged her hand free from his, crossing her arms. "You were going to marry me, Camden, when—" She gasped at the flare of pain in her belly. "When you kept from me that you already had a wife who was with child! If it wasn't for Jasper, I would have married you. I would have become a tainted woman against my knowledge." She laughed without mirth. "But your wife saw to it that I did anyway. She followed you to my district and then spread it all over the neighborhood that I was a light skirt." She swiped at her cheeks. "Do you know how much pain you caused me? I had to leave New York and everything I knew behind because of you."

"Do you know how much pain you caused me?" He echoed her question, hurt flickering in his eyes. "I loved you more than any woman I had ever met. I was going to love you for all your days. You threw it away. And for what? A job as a Harvey Girl?"

"If you really loved me, you would have let me go and never have courted me, asked me to marry you, and pursue me for all my days after I discovered your lies. Am I never to be free of you?" Tacy's limbs trembled, and she grasped Jasper's hand. She was unprepared for the sense of safety his callused hand lent her. Jasper would not allow this man near her . . . he would protect her as he always had.

Camden released a short, bitter laugh. "And yet, you allow my brother to call upon you."

"You sent him to me."

"I'm sure it appears that way." He crossed his arms. "But I never expected him to give up his job for you. I thought he'd be able to convince you to come to me now that my wife is gone."

She gasped. "Mrs. Caffery left you?"

He frowned "She died from pneumonia last year."

"I am so sorry."

"Thank you. She was almost a friend in the end, but you see, now I can offer you my hand in earnest. I have the high-born child my parents required for my inheritance to be released to me, and now, I can mend the brokenness my folly has caused you. I can make your reputation whole again. You can be Mrs. Camden Caffery as we once planned."

No. "I did not leave everything behind, including my name, to become someone that you can create, or destroy, overnight. I am stronger now, and I have built a life that I will never give up for any unworthy man." She dropped Jasper's hand and strode into the Montezuma, never looking back as she had done the moment she found out the truth about Camden.

She hobbled up the stairs to her room, bound her ankle, and in her anger, she dressed for work before realizing her shift didn't start for a few hours. She needed to work, to move and burn away her anger.

With Felicity's permission, she took over a few of her tables, bringing fresh coffee and introducing herself to her guests. Tacy refilled the coffee cup of the gentleman who had been on their walk.

Mr. Lessman eyed her foot. "Seems you have made a remarkable recovery. Did I, perhaps, interrupt your play for Mr. Caffery's hand?"

She pressed her lips into a firm line. She

should have considered how returning to the dining room might look to Mr. Lessman. She would have if she hadn't been so distracted by Camden's arrival. "Can I get anything else for you, Mr. Lessman?"

He wiped his mouth with his overlarge napkin, his mustache leaving a smear of black on the white linen. Did he dye his mustache? She studied his hairline, spying a stain of black dye at the nape of his neck.

"I am quite filled, thank you. It has been quite a while since I've enjoyed such a meal, especially with such exemplary service."

She nodded. "Glad you are happy with the new Montezuma, Mr. Lessman. We aim to please."

"Yes," he grinned under his thick mustache, his eyes crinkling.

He seemed so familiar. A memory flooded her being of her father speaking, begging their landlord for more time on their rent, and the man merely smiled his condolences as one of his men flanking him handed over an eviction notice—a notice that saw her father abandon her before the month was over. She shook her head. This man was far slimmer than her old landlord. *Besides, why would Mr. Wellington be in New Mexico? You are overthinking everything because of Camden.*

"I trust your ankle is fully recovered? Given we are near the hot springs, perhaps you will take advantage of the healing waters during your time off? I myself find them greatly relaxing."

"I'm happy to hear that, sir." She gritted her teeth. She had to find something more original to say, lest he think her surly.

"I was hoping you could post this for me?" He lifted a letter in fine hand.

"Certainly, sir, but there are mail chutes on every—"

"I trust you, my dear." He laughed. "I wanted to seek your opinion. I am looking for a wealthy widow, or pretty heiress. Any suggestions, my dear?"

She gaped at him. "You can hardly believe that I would answer such a thing."

"But you owe me after the trail incident." His voice was teasing, but his eyes held no humor. "It was quite the compromising position I discovered you in with Mr. Caffery, and given you are working already, I can only surmise that the ankle incident was a farce to find you in his arms. I would hate to think of what might have happened if I had not found the both of you."

"I assure you that nothing—"

"I do not require an excuse, merely your help. Isn't that what you Harvey Girls are known for? Your sweet natured service?"

She didn't have to aid him, but Mr. Harvey always wished for his guests to have a good experience . . . and she couldn't afford for anyone to complain about her to Felicity. "Have you made the acquaintance of Mrs. Parker?"

"The woman is ancient."

She couldn't be a day over thirty-five. "Mrs. Richards is also a catch."

"Mayhap I should describe my taste in a wife." His gaze rested on Felicity. "Now, there's a fair lassie."

"She's not rich."

"Pity." He sighed and nodded to the woman in a crimson riding outfit standing in the doorway of the dining room, no doubt waiting for a basket lunch. "Introduce me to Miss Stanley, and the little matter shall be put behind us."

JASPER TOSSED the hay bale into the stall with more force than he had meant, making the mule skitter to the side. He should have gone after Eustacia to ensure she was well and to reassure her that he would protect her from Camden's tendency to threaten people into giving him what he wished.

Jasper seized a brush, intent on grooming every mule until his temper was under control. He might finish all dozen animals before the edge was taken off.

Camden leaned on the stall door, smirking. "So, this is what you choose to do to afford to stay at the resort?"

Jasper ran the brush down the mule's belly as the animal munched on hay. After merely a week under his care, the animals were already looking better. "I have a month of leave owed to me, but I didn't wish to spend my savings if you had me out of a job the moment I returned to work. Thought it best to save myself some grief."

Camden patted the mule's nose. "You always were a cautious sort. I wish I could say I followed your lead in that manner."

Jasper glanced up from cleaning the mule's shoe. His brother *never* complimented him, especially not at his own expense. "What's that supposed to mean?"

"That I didn't just send you here for Eustacia. There is someone else who needed your finding them." Camden slid a folded piece of paper under the mule's saddle pad.

Jasper straightened, senses on alert. Had he missed something? He had certainly been preoccupied with Eustacia.

Camden lifted his finger to his lips, gaze flickering to the stable door. "Now, where is my mule? I booked you for the rest of the day."

"Is that so? Because that is exactly what I have done as well." Miss Stanley paused in the doorway in her crimson gown, staring intently at Camden—as if assessing him.

"Miss Stanley, I meant to address that

with you, but was distracted before I could send a message. The trail is—"

"If it is suitable for a man, then it is suitable for me and my new friend, Mr. Lessman."

Camden paled. "O-of course. Please, let us form our own private party."

"Yes, Miss Stanley. I'll get your mules ready." Retrieving the note would have to wait. But at the fear flickering across Camden's features, he glanced at Mr. Lessman, who was scowling back at Camden, raw anger simmering from his neck to his ears.

CHAPTER SEVEN

Tacy worked until the wee hours, desperate to keep moving. If she kept moving, perhaps it would all fade away like it had last time . . . but she couldn't become Miss Blanche a second time. She'd have to find a new position all together if Camden sought to win her hand by divulging the past.

She approached the last occupied table in the dining room where an exhausted looking mother sat with her toddler with an overzealous finger up his nose. Tacy grimaced as she knew the type of cleaning she had ahead of her. "Can I get you anything else, Mrs. Peterson?"

Her dazed expression fled as if she had just realized Tacy stood before her. The mother quickly made her way out with her son, leaving Tacy a handsome tip and an apologetic smile. She snatched a rag as the two left. Those Caffery men kept coming into her life when she least expected it. If only they would disappear from it as quickly as they arrived . . . but as soon as she had that thought, she amended it to not include Jasper—kind, caring Jasper. *And strong.* The way he carried her down the mountain left little room for the imagination as to his muscular arms. Such a man could protect her from anything.

"Tacy," Camden's deep voice pulled her back in time to when she was young, carefree and in love for the first time. "Won't you walk with me?"

She kept cleaning the table leg.

"I'm leaving the Montezuma. But, before I do, I think we have both been waiting for this conversation for years. Miss Felicity was quite obliging and said Miss Ella will finish righting your tables. I hoped you might spend a moment with me out on the tower's veranda."

She sighed and handed her rag to Ella, who gave her an encouraging smile.

Tacy allowed him to lead her out onto the tower veranda. There were a few elderly couples seated with their opera glasses, observing the night sky, watching for wildlife, and listening to the rise and fall of the cicadas' hum. She guided him to the far wall, seeking a bit of privacy for a talk that would certainly burn any ears listening.

She rested her palms on the rail and studied the beauty of the mountains surrounding the resort. If she looked hard enough, would she see Jasper on his porch with Tom, a lantern swinging overhead as they read their papers in silence?

"Heaven knows what you must think of me. I know how hard it was for you when Jasper disclosed my previous relationship to you."

"You mean, previous marriage that you were still in at the time?" She corrected softly. The anger no longer burned, but the embarrassment was forever fresh. What a fool she had been to think such a wealthy gentleman would have honorable intentions with the former grocer's daughter turned maid in the Irish district? She had been excited by his attention, flattered—perhaps it blinded her to the obvious nature of his courtship. Their gap in stations should have been clue enough.

"I was tricked into an unhappy marriage with her. She trapped me into a union. I was sued for breach of promise, and unless I wed her, I would lose the family's fortune." Camden grasped her hands. "When I met you, I was henpecked and broken after three years under her thumb. Who could fault me for falling in love with a lovely, kind woman who was opposite her in every way?"

She slid her hands from his. "While I pity your situation, you would have made me dishonorable by wedding me . . . immorally making me your second wife." She shook her head. "If you really loved me, you would not have trapped me the way she did you."

His features convulsed. "You dare compare my actions to that of my wife? The woman was unfeeling and cruel."

"And yet you fathered a child with her." *One that you failed to mention at the time.*

"She lied about the first pregnancy." He pressed his lips into a firm line. "Her lie lasted long enough to see you had run away from me forever."

Tears filled her eyes, threatened her lashes, but she would not give in to them. She could feel pity for the man she once loved, but she could never trust him again. "I'm sorry, Camden. There is no hope for us. Ever."

He shook his head. "I will wait for you as long as you wish. I have loved no other but you, Eustacia Gibbs."

"Eustacia Gibbs died long ago, Camden. It is in your best interest to forget there was anything ever between us." *Lord knows I have tried.* "Leave me be."

CAMDEN HAD LAID the world at her feet, and she had rejected him. And Jasper heard every word. He hadn't intended to, but he had been following the man calling himself Mr. Lessman on the ground floor of the tower and had to take a dive into the landscaping to avoid being spotted by him when Tacy and Camden appeared.

After retrieving Camden's folded paper that bore three hastily scrawled words, *"Less is more,"* it didn't take long for Jasper to interpret its meaning. He *had* seen Lessman before. The man had lost weight in prison and dyed his hair, trimming his beard to a mustache, but that grin left little doubt. The man parading as Mr. Lessman was, in fact, the escaped criminal he had been searching for, Mr. Heathcliff Wellington, whose wealth had no doubt shielded him from the law.

Wellington rose from the rocking chair, his gaze focused on the mountains and a smug look on his face—almost as if he too had been waiting and listening for Camden's declaration. Jasper looked where Wellington was staring—a light flashed thrice in the mountains. *A signal? Who is signaling Wellington?*

Wellington strode down the steps and out past the gardens, walking much faster than a man out on a leisurely stroll. If he captured Wellington, Jasper knew his job would be more than safe.

"Jasper?"

He stiffened, whipping around to see Eustacia's tear strewn cheeks, evident in the moonlight, stumbling down the steps of the Montezuma. Wellington halted, as if he heard them. Jasper closed the distance between Eustacia and himself, clapping a hand over her mouth as he pulled her off the corner step into the bushes. "Don't say anything."

Her body trembled under his arm, but she remained silent, trusting him. With the veil of the night sky, they should be protected from Wellington's gaze. At last, the man marched toward the stables, Jasper sighing with relief that her interruption had not cost him finding out what Wellington was about at the Montezuma.

"What is going on?" Eustacia hissed.

"No time to explain. I cannot lose him."

"What on earth is Mr. Lessman doing at

this time of night? He could be hurt, or worse! Someone needs to tell—"

"I don't know, but he is not who he says he is. I have to follow him. I think he might be heading toward the trails." He slowly rose, keeping an eye where Wellington had melted into the shadows. He and Eustacia were too exposed with their backs to the bright Montezuma.

Eustacia grasped his arm. "You don't know the trails well enough to be out of doors at night. If you are following him, I am going with you. I won't have you plunging to your death on my account."

Jasper didn't have the time to argue. He grabbed her hand and ran with her after Wellington, staying far enough away to remain undetected as the man strode past the stables and last outer building toward the trail.

Markham stood at the head of the trail with a saddled mule's reins in hand. "Good evening, Mr. Lessman."

Wellington dropped a coin into the boy's open palm, not enough if he was bribing him, but a tip's amount. The lad surely didn't know what he was about.

Eustacia pulled back. "He's going up the trail without a lantern. He is either insane or desperate. What sort of man do you think he is?"

"One might venture to guess a little of both." He watched Wellington disappear up the trail, counting to ten before he raced forward to his assistant. "Markham! Why did you let him go up the trail at night?"

"It's for science." The boy's eyes shone in the moonlight.

Jasper jerked his head back. "What?"

"He had a special note from Mr. Harvey saying he could use the trails at night for his bat research. He's been going up every few nights."

Good cover with a most likely counterfeit note. But, knowing Wellington's thoroughness, he might actually have convinced Harvey that it was indeed for research. What does he have up in these mountains? Jasper ran into the stable and guided out Mr. Lane's most trustworthy mule and fastened the harness, leading him to the head of the trail. If they were going up the trail, he wanted to be able to fall asleep on the mule's back and trust the mule to get him safely home.

Eustacia eyed the animal. "Jasper . . ."

"You can stay, but this is my job. I need to see that this man is captured and brought to justice."

"Who is he?"

"You may know him as your old landlord. Heathcliff Wellington, of Wellington Sugar."

She sucked in a breath. "I *knew* I recognized him!"

"I need to go. Stay with Markham."

She tilted her neck from side to side, cracking it before reaching for the mule's wiry mane. "Not a chance."

"Very well, but we need to stay as close as we can to him and each other." Jasper set her at the front of the mule and climbed up behind her, wrapping her in his arms and kicking the animal into a trot until they heard the gentle clopping of hooves before them.

He slowed his mount to keep pace at a safe distance. He tapped Eustacia's shoulder and held his finger to his lips. She nodded, understanding the need for silence.

Wellington traveled slowly up the mountain until midway when he turned his mule off the path.

"Do you have any idea where he might be heading?" Jasper whispered as he guided his mule into the woods.

"Mr. Lane mentioned there were trapper buildings out here, but never ventured from the path to find them." Eustacia squinted in the moonlight, shifting to avoid branches.

"Tom has never told me that." His gut clenched.

"Guess he thought it wasn't relevant."

"Or perhaps he had another reason for not telling a Pinkerton." Jasper prayed he was wrong on that front, but he had seen too many good men taken down by Wellington's threats and schemes.

The mule lunged forward as if it were near home.

"Duck!" She gasped, laying against the mule's mane, a cedar branch scraping over Jasper's spine. He grunted against the pain but trusted the mule knew where he was going. Moonlight spilled over a small clearing with a good-sized cabin that looked like it had been built over a hundred years ago, given all the grime covering it, but it looked sturdy enough.

He pulled back on the reins, and, slipping down, helped Eustacia from the mule's back.

Wellington lifted his walking cane and rapped three short beats on the door. It flung open. A giant of a man waved Wellington inside.

Jasper grasped her hand and darted across the clearing. He pressed his back to the wall, Eustacia following suit. He had to find out what was going on inside. He ran along the side of the building, ducking down to avoid being spotted through the filthy window and ran to the back to find a second entrance. He tried it. *Locked. Blast. That would have been too easy.*

Eustacia slipped a hairpin from her coiffure and nudged him over, sticking it in the lock and twisting it until a soft click was heard. She grinned. "My da used to lock the sweets away from Ma and me in a cabinet in his store."

He waited, listening for movement. He exhaled, and turned the knob, slowly swinging the well-oiled door open. He slipped inside and hid behind the back-room's door to hear rustling on the other side.

"Did you get *all* the gold in? I wasn't intending on staying at the Montezuma all this time. I didn't think it would take you so long, or I wouldn't have hired you. I thought you said you were the leader of some gang. The Death Riders, right?"

"Well, it's just me and my pa in the Riders for now, but I know I kept you waiting. I am sorry, sir. When that Pinkerton showed up, I thought the plan was gone for sure. And then there was some trouble breaking into your company's safe. But my pa is an expert—"

"I don't need to hear about your trouble fetching my gold, Grant. I will award you for your extra troubles even though I did have to go through the trouble of making a contingency plan if you failed me." The clinking of gold coins filled the room. "But it looks like I don't need to use it after all as my gold is all here, and I can finally depart the states. Thank God. I am so sick of this climate. What is the point of owning property in Europe under my alias if I don't have the gold to get to it?"

Jasper removed his pistol and strode into the dimly lit room, aiming at Wellington as the other man, he supposed was Grant, dove out the broken window, shattering whatever glass was left. He ignored the young man and kept his gaze trained on his prize. "Wellington, you are under arrest."

CHAPTER EIGHT

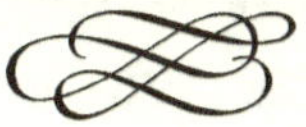

It was nearly one in the morning by the time they reached the Montezuma's lobby. He had a telegram sent to the offices in New York, and while he awaited the answer on what to do with the escaped prisoner, he locked Wellington in the basement of the Montezuma and sent a messenger boy to the sheriff's office in town with a note about the gold sitting in the trapper's cabin. Jasper doubted it was still there with Wellington's accomplice still free, but he had to at least try to have it, and Grant, apprehended.

Camden left within the hour of Wellington's being secured, promising Jasper that he would return his Pinkerton position if he brought back his bride-to-be. Jasper swallowed back the retort that with Wellington's arrest, he didn't need his brother's permission, nor endorsement.

However, as Jasper attempted to rest in the lobby while he waited for further instruction to arrive via telegram, he determined he would remain at the Montezuma for another reason all together. He would muck stalls and commit to back breaking work . . . anything to be by Eustacia's side again. Even if it took years, he would do it to convince the woman he loved that he was *nothing* like his brother.

With dawn's light glowing beyond the mountains and the Harvey staff beginning to swarm about, preparing for guests, he surrendered resting. Jasper strode out to the gardens and picked a nosegay, composing a mental note to accompany them and jotting it down the moment he was able. He sealed the letter and addressed it, *For Miss Blanche.*

He trotted up the stairs, handful of blooms and letter in hand, and paused outside the women's wing door. Should he simply set the flowers and card on the small end table beside the entrance? She would find it when she awoke. He drew in a bracing breath. It was time to wake up the general store owner and see what he could purchase in the way of rings. *Lord, you've granted my dream of finding her. Let her heart be open to me.*

A TAPPING at her window drew Tacy from her deep sleep. She groaned and rolled over in bed. Her roommate was sound asleep after their lengthy conversation about Jasper. *Will that ridiculous bird ever figure out that it is a glass window and not a magical door to a land filled with food?* She plopped her pillow over her head and groaned as the tapping persisted. *Well, it is a Harvey resort, so maybe he is on to something about the food.* She threw aside her pillow, and wrapping her overlarge blue throw around her shoulders, she flung open the window. The bird was nowhere in sight.

"Good morning!" Jasper called down

from below. His hair was wet from a fresh washing, and he was in a fresh emerald shirt and his biscuit colored riding pants. His dimples and broad smile made her heart skip before she realized how she must look.

She gasped and ducked back inside, running her fingers over her hair. It was a mess from their pursuit of Wellington through the trees last night. She wrapped the blanket over her head and leaned out, whispering, "Jasper. What on earth are you doing? It's barely five in the morning."

He laughed. "How else am I supposed to spend time with you when you have work all day?"

She shook her head, chuckling. "Fine. Get a cup of strong coffee for the both of us, and I'll meet you in the gardens."

He winked at her. "Yes, Miss Blanche."

She selected her burgundy gown. The bustle was a bit ostentatious for a simple walk, but what was the point of having a second gown if she didn't wear it? She threw on the ensemble, the bustle giving her a little trouble, but in the end, she managed it. She swept her hair into a pretty coiffure and glanced back down at Violet, rolling her eyes at her friend's ability to sleep through anything.

She snuck out the door of the women's wing, a flash of color catching her eye on the table. She lifted up the small bouquet and the note with her name on it. Her heart pounded as she opened it.

My darling Eustacia, I've dreamt for years of finding you. I don't think you realize how much you touched my heart when we first met. Your kindness and encouragement pushed me to become a Pinkerton when all I thought I was capable of was being in the family business. Because of your sweet heart, I found my own yearning to be close to you. Every day without you has felt like something was missing. My heart would call out to you, and the echo of your encouragement to hold on to my dream to become a Pinkerton made me hold on to a hope of another dream that hardly had a chance to take wing before it was gone—you. These days by your side have been all I have ever longed for, and I pray they will not end.

With all my love,

Jasper

She tucked the letter into her pocket and hurried down the stairs and out to the back gardens, her gaze sweeping for him, finding him seated under a massive, knotted live oak, a cup of coffee in each hand. She sank beside him, reached for the cup he held out to her, and inhaled the tendrils of steam lifting from the brew before sipping the latte, the creaminess sweetening her mouth. The pair enjoyed their coffee in silence, overlooking the mountains as the sun rose. "Thank you for the note."

"I meant every word." He set aside their cups and grasped her hands in his. "Tell me that you want nothing to do with me, and I'll go away."

Violet had told her the same thing. It was one thing for a man to pursue a woman without hope and another to give a man false hope. She was tired of running, but she was even more exhausted from running from her own feelings. As much as she did not wish it, she had fallen for another Caffery man, but he was nothing like his brother. Perhaps it was time to release what she found in her heart into the light. She turned to him, breath catching at the look in his eyes. "To my surprise, I find that I cannot do such a thing . . ."

He squeezed her hands, waiting.

"I didn't want to allow you into my heart, but you have found a way to lower even the strongest of defenses." She laughed. "Perhaps, it might have to do with the fact that you managed to get my dearest friend to speak on your behalf."

"Bless Violet Trent."

He lifted her hand to his lips. The touch sent a spark up her arm, her heart hammering within her breast as he shifted to kneeling and reached into his pocket, lifting out a simple gold ring with a single precious pearl in the center.

"Eustacia Gibbs Blanche. I have loved you from the moment I met you, and though I tried to forget you after I lost all hope of finding you, you were always in my dreams."

It's too soon. We've only just returned to each other's lives! Tacy's mind whispered as her hands clasped to her throat. *But oh, how I wish I could forget the past and say yes.* "How can you possibly know that you love me?"

"It would be impossible for time to quench what I feel for you. All these years apart, I have worked as a Pinkerton diligently, but I never felt completely at home until I found you. You are what I've been searching for, and I know what I want more than anything." He rose, pulling her to standing, towering over her as he grasped her hands in his. "And it is you."

"Jasper . . ." she whispered, too dazed to say much else.

"Take all the time that you need. I expected you wouldn't be able to give me an answer right away." He pressed the ring into the palm of her hand. "But when you look at this ring, know how much I adore you with all of my soul and know that if you accept me, I am yours forever—past, present, and future." He pulled her into his arms. He did not ask for a kiss, but held her as if he were afraid she would disappear again. "I know you don't *need* a husband, but I want you to *want* me to be there for you."

Her eyes welled. "Jasper. My heart wants to say yes, but my head, which has so long kept me from a relationship, needs time to think and see if this is wise. We've only known each other for so short a time." Her fingers trailed down his arm, longing sweeping through her body to become this man's wife. "I don't want to make a decision based on emotions alone."

"I understand. Think on it, my love. You'll have time as I need to bring Wellington to New York to stand trial. I'll return within the week after I settle my affairs in New York. If you find you still need time, I'll work in the stables in order to be near you."

"If I do say yes, it's been so long since I've been in New York . . . I don't know if I have the stomach for the city after living in the West for so long."

His eyes brightened. "If you marry me, I'd give it all up. I have waited too long and searched too far to lose the woman I love now over a job. We could make it work. Maybe they would even allow you to stay on as a Harvey Girl if you wanted to. I could find a new position. Maybe I can set up a Pinkerton office here in Las Vegas. I've heard the sheriff could use any help he can get in this wild territory."

"You would do that for me?"

"I'd do anything for you."

It would be difficult to leave her beloved position as a Harvey Girl if they didn't allow her to stay on as a married woman, but even if they did release her, perhaps it was time to face the past with a man worthy to stand by her side. "Jasper Caffery, there is no need for you to wait for an answer—"

Alarm bells sounded. She whirled around to see smoke billowing from the Montezuma, flames flickering in the windows. She blinked against the sight. Was she dreaming? One glance at Jasper told her she was not having a nightmare. "Dear Lord in heaven. It's happening again!" She moved to run for the building.

He captured her wrist. "Wait! I'm sure they have it under control."

"Like last time? Violet is still asleep! She can sleep through anything." She wrenched herself from his grasp and ran inside, pushing past those evacuating the building. The last Montezuma had been consumed by flames—taking everything of her past life with it. The flames would not take her dearest friend. She threw open the door, Violet still snug under the covers even as the room filled with smoke. She dashed to her side and shook Violet. She didn't respond. Tacy reached for a pitcher of water and threw it into Violet's face. She gasped, her eyes fluttering until she gave into a faint.

"Help!" Tacy cried out as she pulled Violet's arm over her shoulder and stumbled to the door as screams filled the air. Her foot caught and she fell. She closed her eyes against the pain to come, but a strong arm caught her about the waist, breaking their fall.

"I've got you," he whispered. "I've always got you."

CHAPTER NINE

Tacy dropped her water bucket into the ashes and sank to the ground. "It's all gone." Her tears streaked down her cheeks as she thought of her only family photo that her aunt had sent her. She hadn't had time to save it and now, it was lost forever. *I'll never see my parents' faces again.* Tacy swallowed and shook her head. The thought was too much to bear. She'd face the loss, but not now. Not in front of her Harvey sisters, and certainly not in front of the man responsible for it. Wellington sauntered past her, hands cuffed. He sent her a wink as they loaded him in the wagon.

A hand squeezed her shoulder, and Tacy

looked up to find Jasper at her side. "I am so sorry, Eustacia. If I only had brought him to the jail and waited for a telegram there instead of securing him here, he wouldn't have set the fire and—"

"Don't fault yourself. You have a terrible habit of taking on other's acts as if you were responsible for simply not arriving in time. You cannot always be a hero and save all before it is too late. The man was desperate, and he has a history of escaping. Who is to say that he wouldn't have escaped the jail in town?"

He squeezed her hand. "I am loath to leave you, but I must escort Wellington with the sheriff to the jail and see him in chains and behind bars." He pressed a kiss to her forehead, earning surprised looks from the girls. "I'll be back as soon as I can, and we can discuss the future."

"Ladies?" Miss Rosehill, the manager's daughter, called to them. "I spoke with the hotel manager down the road, and he's already set aside two rooms for us ladies to use while we await Mr. Harvey's telegram, giving us our orders." She looked to Violet.

"I hope you don't mind. You were not feeling up to the task, and if I didn't act quickly, it would have been filled from our guests and I—"

"You are a wonder, Amelia Rosehill." Violet patted Amelia's hand, her voice raspy from the smoke. "I appreciate your help."

Having no items to pack, the girls clung to one another as they climbed into the wagons the townsfolk had brought. They sat in silence until they reached the bottom of the foothill, and the town's only remaining hotel that was already milling with misplaced guests. The girls plodded into the dusty establishment where servers were ready with trays of coffee and tea for the ladies and guests, directing all to the piles of baked goods that awaited them in the parlor. Tacy secured a rather dry looking scone and sat with the girls for the next hour as each took a turn cleaning up in the shared bathroom upstairs.

The proprietor touched Tacy's arm and handed her an envelope. "You the head girl? This is from Mr. Harvey."

She didn't bother correcting him and

took the missive to Violet. She broke the seal with shaking hands. Tacy rested her head on Violet's shoulder, sighing as she braced herself for their instructions.

"Mr. Harvey sends his sincerest apologies. He doesn't wish you ladies to fear for your waitress positions as he has provided a list of Harvey House restaurants for you all to choose from with several positions available," Violet announced in the cramped hotel parlor. "I'll copy the list and set it on the writing desk in the corner. Line up and write your name in the blank space next to your preferred Harvey House location."

Tacy waited until all of the Harvey Girls had lined up before she strode to the back of the line next to Amelia Rosehill.

"Where are you looking to go?" Amelia asked, biting her lip as she looked down the long line of her fifteen Harvey sisters. "I would like to stay close to here because of family, but I don't think there is much chance of that unless I find another position in town to support us. . . but I doubt I could."

"True." Tacy nodded. "All the good jobs are taken by town girls."

"It's a shame for you too, though, because it's likely that you won't get another second waitress position with such short notice. You'll have to start as a standard waitress again just like me," Ella added as she joined them with a sigh. "Who knows how long it will take to get back on top." She bent down and scribbled her name next to a small town sixty miles southeast. Tacy perused the list. Only one position remained where Ella had signed her name. *Valley Mills, Texas. Might be nice.*

"Tacy?" Violet whispered. "Jasper asked to see you. He is waiting in the cedar grove behind the church."

She paused with the pen in hand. She had been making choices for herself for so long . . . it would be easy to jot her name down and change the direction of her life once more. But Jasper's actions had proven again and again that he put her first. If it came down to it, she would trade her apron for a veil—for Jasper alone.

After securing Wellington and charging him with the burning of the Montezuma, Jasper paced in the trees behind the church, hat in hand. Despite his reasons for becoming a trail guide, he had come to enjoy life in the West and did not wish to leave, even if it meant resigning from his dream job in New York. But, with the resort in ashes and Wellington in custody, he needed to see what Eustacia had in mind.

Tacy strode through the trees, her soot covered gown a stark reminder of all she had lost.

He reached out his arms to her, and she melted into him, head against his chest. She groaned. "Oh, Jasper. What are we going to do?"

We. He liked the sound of that. "Well, for starters, I think *we* should get married."

She lifted her gaze to him. "That fact did not change. What I meant was, where are we to live? We never got to that part of our conversation."

"Despite being a Caffery . . . my brother

has the whole of the estate, thanks to my father's will. So, I need a job right away. I was thinking of opening that office."

"But, if we marry right away, Camden surely will keep you from opening a Pinkerton agency here."

"It will be hard for him to succeed with that now that I have Wellington." He nodded. "But, if that happens, I will follow wherever you want to go next for your position. Surely Mr. Harvey will not refuse to have you as a Harvey Girl, even married, given all you have been through and the years you have dedicated to his chain of restaurants."

"I believe you are right." She worried her bottom lip. "There is a position at Valley Mills at the new Harvey House. How do you feel about Texas? Would you want to set up a private detective agency there? Surely, they would have just as much need of your services as they do here."

"Done." He grinned down at her. "When do we leave?"

She laughed. "There's a train I can be on

tomorrow, but we can't rightly ride off to Valley Mills unwed."

"Then how about we get married today? We are already at a church. We might as well take advantage of it."

She glanced up at the pretty blue church, laughing. "I suppose we are." She placed her hand in his. "I'm afraid I'm not much of a bride covered in soot."

"Soot or not, you are the loveliest woman I have ever met." He wrapped his hands about her waist and whirled her about before setting her feet atop his boots as he kissed her soundly.

She giggled and gently pushed him away. "Now, Mr. Caffery. We can't have any of that now or people might think something."

"Think that we are in love? Because I know I am." He led her up the white steps into the pretty blue church. "How did I ever manage to win your heart?"

"Your name was always carved into my heart. I simply didn't know it until now." She grasped his face gently between her hands, pulling him down to her. Her lips met his, their passion growing with every breath until they broke apart with a laugh. "I love you, Jasper Caffery."

"Not as much as I love you, Eustacia Gibbs."

She giggled. "Time will tell who does indeed love the other the most."

A few moments were all it took for Tacy and Jasper to be bound for eternity. Jasper placed his left hand at the nape of her neck and the other at her waist, whispering, "Thank you for trusting me—for loving me. I promise to love you forever, Mrs. Caffery." He pressed his lips to hers, smiling all the while before he lifted her and spun her about—their hearts together at last.

AUTHOR'S NOTE

Dear Reader, if this is your first time reading about the Harvey Girls, know that they did indeed exist. In the 1880s, there were not many respectable jobs for women, so when Englishman Fred Harvey created his chain of fine dining restaurants along the Atchison, Topeka, and Santa Fe railroads, single women without an education, or in need of earning their own way, were given a chance to earn an honest wage without the speculation that they offered anything else but food as a service.

With Mr. Harvey's strict rules about the waitress's code of conduct, the women were given their independence while still maintaining their good name and place in society under the protective, fatherly arm of Fred Harvey. These extraordinary, brave women became known as the Harvey Girls, the ladies who tamed the Wild West with fine china, good pie, and exceptional service with complete propriety.

The first Montezuma resort did indeed burn down. After a year of rebuilding with new architects, the second resort opened for only four short months before the "fireproof" hotel burned to the ground with only a partial stone structure remaining. For the purposes of this story, I had Wellington be the culprit behind the fire and moved up the timeline by a few weeks. Fred Harvey lost no time and re-built the Montezuma a third time, dubbing it *The Phoenix.* The resort eventually reverted to its former name, though, so their superstitious guests would not think it likely to burn down again. It did not, and you can still see the third Montezuma building today.

I did take some small liberties with the Montezuma resort, but I did attempt to stay as close as possible with the historical pictures and references available for the second Montezuma. There was a burro trail. I have never ridden a burro, *but* I have ridden a mule down into the Grand

Canyon, a terrifying and thoroughly enjoyable adventure that I want to repeat in the future. I thought I might be able to give better authenticity if I made them mules.

If you enjoyed the collection, I would love it if you could write a brief review, or leave a star rating, on your favorite bookish site. Every review is golden, and if you tag me on social media, I'll do my best to repost, or comment on your post!

Thank you for your continued support and happy reading, friends!

Grace Hitchcock is the award-winning author of multiple historical novels and novellas, including the American Royalty, Best Laid Plans, and Aprons & Veils series. She holds a Master's in Creative Writing and a Bachelor of Arts in English with a minor in History. Grace lives in South Louisiana with her husband, Dakota, sons, and daughter in a farmhouse that is always filled with the sounds of sweet little footsteps running at full speed. When not writing, chasing her toddlers, or tending to her chickens and golden and labrador retrievers, she's baking something delightful and can usually be found with a book clutched in her fist.

APRONS & VEILS
BOOK ONE

The Finding of Miss Fairfield

GRACE HITCHCOCK

CHAPTER ONE

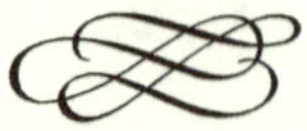

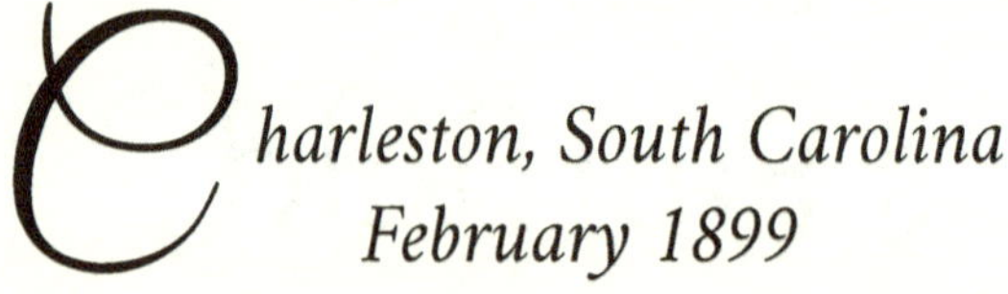

Charleston, South Carolina
February 1899

SOPHIA FAIRFIELD'S heart skipped at the sight of Mother holding a damp handkerchief to her eyes as Father and his business partner, Prescott Payne, stood before the floor-length windows facing Charleston Harbor with their heads together, speaking in low, somber tones over the crackling of the fireplace. They halted their whispering when they caught sight of her standing in the second-floor East drawing room doorway, her reticule dangling from her fingertips with her box of new poetry, papers, and pencils propped on her hip. "Mother? What's wrong?"

Mr. Payne stepped forward, his emerald eyes capturing hers in a most disconcerting fashion. Grinning down at her, he ran his hand over his neatly trimmed gray beard. "My dearest Sophia, I've spoken with your father and mother, and they have wholeheartedly given us their blessing to wed."

Sophia's stomach dropped, her limbs aching to bolt from the parlor as the grandfather clock in the corner sounded the noon hour. Her gaze darted to Mother's elated face. Sophia had only accepted Mr. Payne's suit last month as a courtesy to her father, intending on ending things once Mr. Payne saw that they were ill-suited for one another, given he was over twice her age, but he had apparently not understood her subtle hints for him to cease his efforts. *Or not even cared, given he sought my father's answer instead of my own.*

"Is my darling bride-to-be speechless at

last?" Prescott held his hand out to her, inviting her to join him.

Bride-to-be? The box slipped from her grasp, the items scattering about the floor. She dropped to her knee to retrieve them, but Father crossed the room and seized her arm.

"Leave it for Belle." He waved forward the petite maid standing beside the tea service.

Sophia sent her friend an apologetic smile as Father drew her away into the gilded parlor. Though a small room, gold leaf adorned the crown molding and the ornate medallion with the gold and crystal chandelier in the center of the room that illuminated the platinum wall coverings that perfectly matched the opposite West parlor room. Mother had to have a matching set of French chandeliers of her own after her visit to her sister's in New York.

"I have already accepted his hand on your behalf, daughter. You will wed as soon as you choose the day. We were just discussing the arrangements right before you returned home from your little shopping expedition on King Street."

Perhaps I can reason with Father when Prescott departs? But one glance at the pride radiating from her father, she knew it would be hopeless and she would never have the courage to stand against him. Like every time before, she would wilt beneath his crushing will despite her best arguments. She glanced down at her ring finger. She had been fortunate he had never pressed her into a marriage before now . . . but she supposed being the seventh, homeliest child of nine had something to do with it, and now that her youngest and prettiest sisters had wed at Christmas, she should have suspected she was next.

Mr. Payne captured her hand and slid a gold ring with a ruby cushioned by a pearl on either side onto her shaking finger. "What a lovely bride you will be, my dear. I am a fortunate man indeed to have found three women in one lifetime whom I have loved." He kissed her fingertips, his bushy mustache brushing against them and making her jerk back her hand. He narrowed his gaze for a half second before laughing.

Her? A lovely bride? She had been told far too often to keep her bangs trimmed and tidy to hide her high hairline and scolded more often than not for reading too late as it made her eyes habitually shadowed. No one in this family had ever accused her of being a beauty, except perhaps her youngest sister Jane. But Jane was the sweetest of the Fairfield daughters. Maybe it was because of her plainness, Sophia had never thought she would be required to marry. It would have required too much financially of her father to make a good match with a handsome suitor. She worried her bottom lip. Prescott, though twice her age, had retained his charm and could have had any of the society widows. *What has Father offered him to lure him into a match?*

"My second wife was a widow, so I have forgotten how you young brides can be with your wedding nerves," Mr. Payne said to her, conspiratorially elbowing Father.

Mother had the decency to blush while

Father joined in the bawdy laughter, slapping Mr. Payne on the shoulder.

She swallowed back her protest over their assumption that she would marry Mr. Payne, but she could not broach the subject while *he* was in the home. She would have to do battle in secret. She had never stood up to Father's demands before, but her parents had not set their sights solely on marrying her off before. She studied the ruby and all that was tied to it. She twisted it around her finger.

Mother grasped Sophia's hand and admired the gem before turning her bright smile up at Prescott. "It is magnificent. Well done, Mr. Payne. We will make the announcement at Sophia's birthday dinner party tonight. My daughter's engagement to Prescott Payne on her twenty-fifth birthday will be a surprise and delight to all who attend. I would love for Sophia to have a June wedding, but it is rather far away."

Sophia gripped the back of the settee to ground herself. *Please Lord, give me the courage to speak with my father and be victorious just this once. I cannot lose when there is so much at stake.* Now that her siblings were married, she was supposed to have this time to herself—to enjoy being the only daughter in the Fairfield house, to spend her days studying and tutoring her nieces and nephews, as well as the dear girls at the orphanage.

"Two months will be more than sufficient to plan a wedding fit for American royalty," Prescott replied, dismissing Mother's suggestion without so much as an apology. He snatched up his burgundy planter's hat and cane from the settee and turned on his boot's heel to face Sophia. "I must depart to dress for our engagement party, but know that I am counting the minutes until we wed, my sweet girl."

Then you will be counting forever if I have my way. She managed a weak smile, willing herself to be silent until they were alone. For if she did indeed lose this battle, she did not want Prescott to think of her as a spineless woman, even if everyone else in this family thought it was true. She waited for the downstairs front door to close behind him and crossed the drawing room to the window, watching the happy couples and families in carriages passing below her on East Bay Street. She closed her eyes against the sight, silence greeting her ears. She ached for the days when the house was filled with the sounds of her siblings running up and down the stairs, laughter filling the home—no matter how much they teased her for her looks and her nose always being stuck in a poetry book.

"Don't you think it is a little soon for me to consider marriage to Mr. Payne?" Sophia looked tentatively up at her father. "Not that I am not honored by having a gentleman in such high standing interested in me, but we hardly know one another."

"It certainly is not. For some reason, he considers you attractive even though you are practically an old maid and well," he motioned at her with one hand.

"Ernest." Mother cleared her throat. "What your father means is that he's far more established than any other suitor you have ever entertained."

"At fifty-five, one would hope for establishment, but I've only entertained the suitors my sisters rejected who only wanted to call upon me in order to become better acquainted with Father and his shipping industry," Sophia mumbled, running her fingertip over the wavy glass, longing to be out of doors, even if it was freezing, to be away from his oppressive gaze. At least on the portico she could breathe and pretend not to be trapped by her parents' expectations.

Father sighed and gently grasped her wrist, turning her toward him. "You are trying my patience with your protests, my dear. You must admit I have been more than indulgent of your sisters' choices in suitors, and your lack of interest in suitors in the past, but you cannot stay in my household forever. And if you will not pick a gentleman who suits your fancy and who actually wishes to marry you, I will."

Mother rested a staying hand on Sophia, quieting her protest. "Sophia, you know Prescott could have his pick of any widow in Charleston and yet, he has chosen you, and we couldn't be happier with the match."

She lowered her head, her cheeks

flaming with suppressed anger at her helplessness. "I am well aware of that fact, but you see, I didn't choose him. *Father* did. And how on earth he could expect that I would be happy with a man better suited to be my aging uncle than my husband, I'll never know."

Mother gasped. "Sophia Bird Fairfield! Such an outburst is not to be borne. Apologize to your father at once."

Father held up his hand, the diamond in his gold ring on his little finger shimmering. "No, she's right. I was the one urging you to accept my friend as a suitor in the first place, and I'm the one who has accepted his hand for you." He took Sophia's hand in his with a tenderness she had not felt in years. "I've always had your best interests in mind, which sometimes means I have to make the difficult decisions for you. As a little girl, you trusted me to take care of you, but after that bout with scarlet fever that weakened you, I had to be, what appeared at the time, callous in my choices for you." He stroked her cheek with the back of his hand. "All I ask is that you trust me again, Sophia, and know I will do what is right for you."

"I do trust you, but am I never to have a voice? Or would you have me follow your will on this as I have done for everything else in my life because it's easier than disagreeing with you?" She bit her lip at the hardness returning to his eyes. Sophia's will waivered as it always did in the face of his disapproval, and he knew it.

"Your siblings have all made marriages of advancement. This would not only make me happy, but I've spoken with your brothers Elton, Thomas, *and* Robert. They all agree that Prescott is a most advantageous match for the family. As my business partner, and a gentleman of great means in his own right, I know Prescott has stature among not only all of Charleston, but nationally. He will take care of you in the manner you are accustomed to and will give you all that your heart desires." He gave her a little smirk. "I imagine he would provide you with a library full of every poetry book you have ever dreamed of possessing."

Mother nodded, placing her arm about

Sophia's petite waist. "And more importantly, Prescott expressed to me how much he adores you."

"We have only been seeing each other for a month . . ." Sophia shook her head, incredulous at the news. She could count on her right hand the weeks he had called upon her. "No, it hasn't even been a month because he was out of the city for a week, so how on earth could he possibly *adore* me?"

"Sometimes, it only takes a day." Mother smiled up at Father. "It only took a moment for us to fall in love." She stroked Sophia's cheek, tucking a stray flaxen lock behind her ear. "A love for Prescott will come. Trust us. Just give it time."

SEATED in the middle of the massive mahogany dining table with Mr. Payne on her left, Sophia felt on display in her copper silk creation from Worth with its daring neckline, which Mother had insisted upon. And seeing as Mother would broach no argument, Sophia defiantly had her bangs braided back to reveal her high hairline, despite her mother's expressed disapproval.

Sophia glanced to her right where Mother was making small talk with her dinner guests across the table, her siblings and their spouses sprinkled throughout the group of close friends. Sophia struggled to keep her expressions from reflecting the dread she had been attempting to mask all evening in the flickering light of the Girandoles, their four candlesticks further illuminated in the convex looking glasses.

Smoothing her silk skirt, she attempted to slow her racing heart and focused on the melodies of the string quartet. Mother hated lulls in conversation, so she always had soft music flowing through the foyer from the downstairs parlor during dinner parties, which sometimes made for a noisy dinner, but for once, Sophia did not mind as it gave her time to collect her thoughts. How had this afternoon gone so differently than she had hoped?

When she had broached the topic of becoming an English tutor for the other young ladies of Charleston, as well as continuing her work at the orphanage, both her parents scoffed at her offering—even though she had been the one to teach her nieces and nephews how to not only read but enjoy the study of poetry. While her parents saw her tutoring in the orphanage little more than wasted charity, Sophia knew she was making a difference as two of her charges, who were aging out of the orphanage, obtained positions as English teachers.

If she wasn't allowed to tutor, what other choice did she have? According to her father, she needed to have her own home at once—to be provided for as a gentlewoman. Without the option of a position, she was left with no other choice. *Lord, give me direction. Send me someone else! Or give me a way out of this marriage.*

"You are radiant this evening, my darling."

His deep voice awoke Sophia from her reverie, and she looked to her intended. He was a well-preserved gentleman for his age and if they had time together, perhaps she could indeed become friends with him even if the thought of sharing a life with him made her stomach turn. "Thank you, Mr. Payne."

"I believe it would be appropriate now for us to address one another by our given names. After all, we are betrothed," he grinned, his eyes sparkling in the candlelight that further shadowed his crow's feet.

"Very well, Prescott." She took a substantial bite from her sweet potato roll to avoid saying anything else. The sweet bread caught in her throat, and she released a series of strangled coughs that had her reaching for her water glass and her mother shooting her a scowl.

"I wish you did not feel so nervous around me, *Sophia*." Prescott chuckled, returning his attention to his mushroom soup.

"Nervous? Why ever would you think that?" Sophia cleared her throat and took a spoonful of soup but missed her mouth slightly. She snatched up her napkin and dabbed her reddening cheek.

His hand slid over the tablecloth and encased hers. "Because, besides almost choking on your bread, I can feel your hand trembling." He smiled. "A sweet trait for a bride-to-be, but as your future groom, I would like a bit more from you than a chaste kiss on the hand."

"More?" Her voice cracked. *What is he asking?*

He leaned toward her, his eyes rolling appreciatively over her gown. "A kiss at the end of the evening is more than proper . . . and I do not mean on the cheek." He slowly ran his finger over her wrist in small circles. "You have no need to fear me. I will be a good and gentle husband to you."

A kiss. Simple to a man with two wives before her, but she had always longed to share her first kiss with a man she loved. She carefully withdrew her hand and dipped her head, sensing Prescott stiffening beside her at her silent refusal.

Father rose from the head of the dining room table, clearing his throat and lifting his glass. Prescott caught her hand under the table and Sophia's cheeks flamed as she once more slipped her hand away and folded them demurely on her lap. They were not married yet and she had no such intentions of allowing him *any* liberties, no matter his disapproval. *You can do this, Sophia.* She glanced across the table toward her childhood friend, Beatrice Hawthorne, and sent her a small smile, wishing she had the chance to tell Beatrice before the announcement even though she had no intention of following through with the match.

"Ladies and Gentlemen, may I please have the honor of your attention?" Father clinked his glass with a spoon. "I have asked you here tonight, not simply as a gathering of friends and family, but in celebration of a long-anticipated matter." He smiled down at Sophia and Prescott, sending murmurs throughout the dinner party. "Most of you know, the Payne family and the Fairfields have done business together for many years and tonight, our bond deepens. Tonight, it gives me great joy to announce the engagement of my daughter to Prescott Payne."

The room erupted with applause and cheers. Chairs scraped against the oak floor as her sisters and friends rushed to wish her well and congratulated Prescott. Despite her tumultuous heart, she smiled and accepted their warm wishes, endeavoring to catch the eye of Beatrice, but her friend remained seated, her gaze fixed on her crystal glass with heated cheeks. Sophia thought she could detect tears glistening in Beatrice's eyes, but before she could reach her, Prescott threaded Sophia's arm through his and led her up the curving stairs to the entertaining rooms, only pausing once they were in the center of the East drawing room. The Persian rug had been rolled up and stowed away, allowing for dancing. With a nod of his head, he signaled the quartet, who must have taken the servant's stairs during the announcement to meet them.

He bowed to her as they began to play a waltz. "May I have this dance?"

Feeling all eyes trained on them, Sophia curtsied, allowing him to take her into his arms. His gentle touch upon her waist brought forth a sigh from a group of ladies as Prescott guided Sophia past, her skirts whirling as he effortlessly moved them about the floor in perfect time, his eyes never leaving hers. His attentiveness almost made her think they had a chance of happiness, if this was somehow the Lord's will. But as the music faded into silence, Prescott led her off the dance floor and the spell vanished from his eyes as guest after guest came up to reiterate their happiness of the couple's coming nuptials.

Jane drew her into an embrace, her blue eyes bright with unshed tears. "Dearest sister, I am ever so happy for you both." She rested her hand on her abdomen. "Marriage is such a boon, and children are a blessing that fills one to overflowing with joy." She kissed Sophia's cheek, whispering, "I know you are uncertain of the whole business, but truly, I think you will be happy."

"Thank you, Jane." She squeezed her sister's hands as the next couple pressed forward. She longed to have a talk with her sister, but if she approved of the match, she might inadvertently give away Sophia's true feelings on the matter. No. It was best to keep her feelings tucked away.

But with every well-wisher, Sophia's

heart grew heavier. *Lord help me to get through tonight. Give me direction.*

"Sophia." Beatrice hissed, tugging her arm from behind.

Sophia was about to excuse herself from Prescott, but found he was so engrossed with a fellow businessman, she could easily slip away without notice. She grasped Beatrice's arm and accepted the silk shawl from her ever-attentive maid, Belle. Sophia smiled her thanks and guided Beatrice out onto the portico, inhaling the gentle breeze from the bay rustling through the magnolia leaves and palmetto branches. She leaned against the thick rail, drawing in the lights dancing in the harbor from anchored vessels. Perhaps there was a captain in need of a ship's boy? She was scrawny enough. Or perhaps a handsome captain who needed a bride and wouldn't mind if she wished to spend her time teaching and reading?

"I should have been told." Beatrice crossed her arms against the chill.

She reluctantly turned away from the ships and the wealth of imagination they offered her. "Please forgive me for not telling you sooner, Beatrice. I would have . . . if I had known of my family's intentions."

Beatrice pinched the bridge of her nose, scowling. "Didn't you just tell me three days ago you were going to dismiss him?" She motioned toward Prescott and his ring on Sophia's finger. "And now you are to marry him in a matter of months. What happened?"

Sophia drew her silk shawl over her arms. "What I always feared would happen. My entire life I have been groomed to be a wife. I am not allowed to work. I cannot even travel alone without a maid to accompany me and even to travel *with* a maid, I must have my father's blessing, which he never gives." She met her friend's gaze. "I'm trapped by society and my father's rules. I have no other option because, in my father's eyes, I'm his frail little girl that needs to be looked after by a strong, wealthy man."

Beatrice shrugged, pulling at her gloves to return them to above her elbows. "I could've told you that, but I knew the only way you'd realize the truth was for something like this to happen, or better yet, you'd actually fall in love." She nodded toward Prescott. "But I thought if you didn't become madly in love with Prescott, I wouldn't have minded so much as I would've enjoyed consoling him."

"Beatrice! Some things should not be jested about."

"I am not jesting. I would be honored if he came to call on me. He's everything you could ever want in a man," Beatrice sighed as she gazed hungrily at Prescott. "If you'd only open your mind, you'd see what a good man he is and that he's been trying so hard to capture your hand this entire month. You cannot do better than Prescott Payne, and I suggest you take your focus off of yourself and your *feelings*. We aren't all as fortunate as you to have a wealthy suitor. So, try not to make any impetuous decisions, Sophia. Think of your family and your future." She glanced across the room, "Now, if you'll excuse me, I need to make my own future secure."

Stunned, Sophia followed her friend inside and leaned against the fireplace mantel as Beatrice wove through the crowd to Mr.

Steward's side, an elderly single gentleman of seventy with considerable means.

"My stepfather is the most favored man alive to have captured another angel for a bride," a deep voice murmured behind her.

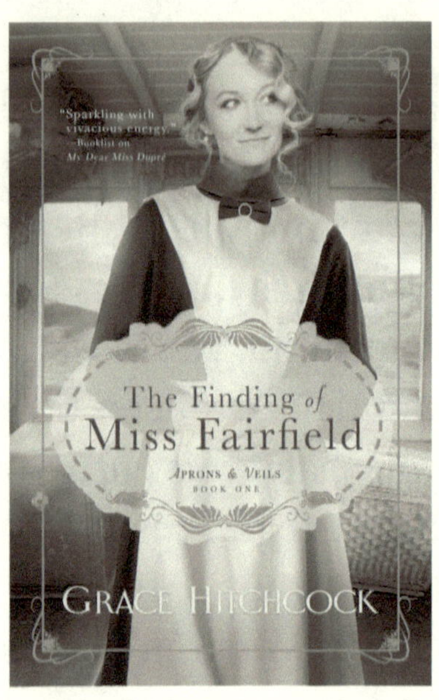

The Harvey Girls Story Continues in Book One of the Aprons & Veils Series, The Finding of Miss Fairfield By Grace Hitchcock.

Sign Up for Grace's Newsletter!

Keep up to date with Grace's news on book releases and giveaways by signing up for her email list at GraceHitchcock.com

---

FREE from Grace Hitchcock

New Orleans, 1895

Colette Olivier, a young widow who married out of obligation, finds herself at the end of her mourning period and besieged with suitors out for her inheritance. With her pick of any man, she is drawn to an unlikely choice.

The Widow of St. Charles Avenue by Grace Hitchcock
a Second Chance Brides Novella
GraceHitchcock.com

Scan to Claim Your FREE Novella

More in your favorite series . . .

Forced into a betrothal with a widower twice her age, Charleston socialite, Sophia Fairfield is desperate for an escape. Much to her dismay, Sophia finds herself falling in love with the wrong gentleman—a man society would never allow her to marry, given Sophia was supposed to be his new stepmother. The only way to save Carver from ruin is to run away, leaving him and all else behind to become a Harvey Girl waitress at the Castañeda Hotel in New Mexico.

The Finding of Miss Fairfield by Grace Hitchcock
Aprons & Veils #1
A Friends-to-Lovers Runaway Bride RomCom

With a hope for belonging, Belle Parish leaves her position as a maid in Charleston to travel to New Mexico to become a mail-order bride. Colt Lawson's letters hold great promise, but something does not add up. Belle flees straight into the Castañeda Hotel Harvey House. Giving up the prospect of marrying, she focuses on her role as a Harvey Girl waitress until a strong Texas Ranger rides into her life.

The Pursuit of Miss Parish by Grace Hitchcock
Aprons & Veils #2
A Mail-Order Bride RomCom

Tanner Sterling has hunted his last bounty. As a new foreman, he wasn't expecting to rescue a sweet Harvey Girl from a raging river his first day. But, when he sees her on a wanted poster, he knows hunters will be coming for her. Despite wanting to hang up his past along with his gun belt, Tanner will do anything to protect her from the coming storm . . . even if he has to claim the bounty himself.

The Vanishing of Miss Victoria by Grace Hitchcock
Aprons & Veils #4
An Enemies-to-Lovers RomCom

www.ingramcontent.com/pod-product-compliance
Lightning Source LLC
LaVergne TN
LVHW090954080826
845145LV00003B/1001

* 9 7 8 1 9 7 0 6 7 5 0 3 0 *